After Spike began eating, Toby said, "Spike, if you wanted to hide a shoe, where would you hide it?"

Spike blinked around the room. "Under the bed."

Toby shook his head. "First place anyone would look for a shoe. *I'd* hide it in a shoe store."

"Oh, yeah," Spike chewed thoughtfully, "like hiding a needle in a haystack."

"No," said Toby, "like hiding a piece of hay in a haystack. *I'd* hide a needle in a sewing box."

Faintly, they could hear music from Fantazyland.

"Spike, if you had to hide a kid, where would you hide him? *I'd* hide him anywhere there are lots of other children."

Toby continued to look at Spike. After a moment, very cheerfully, Toby said, "Hey, Spike! We going to Fantazyland today? Nice day for it. . . ."

"Fact is, kid," Spike said; "we are."

... GOT MORE THAN HE BARGAINED FOR.

Other novels by Gregory Mcdonald

WHO TOOK TOBY RINALDI?

Gregory Mcdonald

A DELL BOOK

Published by
Dell Publishing Co., Inc.
1 Dag Hammarskjold Plaza
New York, New York 10017

Dell ® TM 681510, Dell Publishing Co., Inc.

ISBN 0-440-19542-X

Reprinted by arrangement with G.P. Putnam's Sons.

Printed in Canada

First Dell printing—October 1981

*Dedicated to several women
I have been lucky to know,
who have taught me from their
courage, strength and wisdom.*

One

"Is the Ambassador there?"

"I'm sorry. The Ambassador is in conference."

"This is Mrs. Rinaldi, Sylvia. Calling from California."

"Oh, I'm sorry, Mrs. Rinaldi. One moment."

Across the airport corridor from her was a bookstore. People with luggage at their feet, some with packages under their arms, were browsing. Moving themselves and their luggage a few steps, stopping, taking a book off the rack, looking at it, perhaps keeping it in hand, perhaps putting it back, moving another few steps, sometimes moving back to take a book they had already returned to the rack: they were doing a dance, really, a slow dance with books as partners.

"Christina?"

She turned to face the inside of the phone booth.

"Are you having a good time at your tennis camp? How's your serve coming?"

"Teddy," she said. "What's the change of plans? I'm at the airport in San Francisco now."

"What change of plans?"

"Toby wasn't on the plane."

From behind his desk in his United Nations office, Ambassador Teodoro Rinaldi glanced expressionlessly at the three members of his staff sitting comfortably around the room, notes and note pads on their laps. None looked at him. Unrealistically, politely, they were trying to grant the Ambassador a private conversation with his wife.

In his own head, a distant alarm bell sounded—just

once. It was the sound he had been half expecting every moment of his professional life.

Even in front of his own staff he must be careful in what he was to say now.

The Ambassador said to his wife, "Tell me about it."

"Flight 203," she said, "New York to San Francisco, Brandt Airlines, arriving three fifty-three P.M."

"Yes. . . ." he said.

"They were supposed to deliver Toby to the V.I.P. lounge. I was there in plenty of time."

"I see."

"They didn't bring Toby to the lounge. The plane arrived. I watched the electronic board. I waited a half hour, forty minutes, thinking there might be a baggage delay. No Toby. What plane is he on?"

The Ambassador looked at his watch. It was five eighteen in California. His wife's alarm had been growing for almost an hour. She was doing well.

He said, "There had been no change of plans, as far as I know."

"But, Teddy. There must have been."

"What have you done so far?" he asked.

"I explained the situation to the head stewardess in the V.I.P. lounge. She brought me to the manager. The Brandt Airlines manager here. A Mr. Swenson. He was very kind. He was able to tell me Toby's plane reservation was canceled. Last night. In New York."

"He said what?"

"Why didn't you have someone tell me?"

The Ambassador said, "Hold on one moment." He depressed the intercommunication-system button on his desk and spoke to his secretary: "Sylvia, what plane was my son, Toby, on to California?"

"Brandt Airlines Flight 203," she answered. "Arriving San Francisco International at three fifty-three this afternoon."

"Would you please call Mrs. Brown at the Residence and confirm that Toby got off all right?" From across his office, the Embassy's chief of Public Relations, Ria Marti, looked up at him sharply. The Ambassador said evenly, "There seems to be some delay."

The secretary said, "Yes, sir."

Into the phone the Ambassador said to his wife, "I'm sure there's just some mix-up, Christina. I'm having Sylvia call Mrs. Brown."

"Teddy, Mr. Swenson—The Brandt Airlines manager here—wasn't able to tell me what plane Toby is on. He said the reservation was simply canceled. He said there is no reservation for Toby Rinaldi on any Brandt Airlines flight today, tomorrow, whenever. . . ."

"The airlines are very careful about these things. . . ." The Ambassador knew that in talking he simply was filling up empty air. He was confronted with two sets of facts that did not jibe. He said, "Hold on." The light of another telephone line on his desk was flashing.

Through the intercom, Sylvia said, "Mrs. Brown is on three, Mr. Ambassador."

"Thank you." The Ambassador put his wife's call on hold and pushed the button for extension 353.

"Mrs. Brown? Did Toby get off all right?"

"Of course."

"You got him to the airport on time?"

"Plenty of time. He even insisted on my sittin' down with a cup of tea. A born diplomat, like his father, sir, I'll tell you."

"Did someone meet you at the airport?"

"Yes, sir. A young man. From the airlines."

"Did Toby have Mrs. Rinaldi's telephone number at the tennis camp in California?"

"Oh, he had everything, sir. The airlines sent a complete packet, you know, I had to fill out, for sending a child alone on an airplane. Names, addresses, numbers to call, allergies, if any, if the child is a particular eater, please state, Toby's name tag, everything."

"What did the name tag say, Mrs. Brown?"

"It was from the airlines, sir. Well, it said, printed out, you know, I'M BRANDT AIRLINES CAPTAIN and then I had printed in TOBY RINALDI . . . FLYING FLIGHT 203 TO SAN FRANCISCO and then today's date, sir. It had a picture of an airlines captain's hat in the upper left-hand corner."

"What was the last you saw of Toby?"

"Why, going through the security systems, sir. Toby was real disappointed he couldn't make the warning buzzer go off. Mr. Ambassador, there isn't anything wrong, is there?"

"No," he said too quickly.

"How could there be?" she said. "He was in the charge of airlines people. If they don't know how to put someone on an airplane, I don't know who would. His mother was meeting him in San Francisco."

"Quite right," the Ambassador said. "You haven't heard from the airlines or anyone else since you got home?"

"Well, I did, sir. The carpet-cleaning company. You know, the company that picked up the carpets for cleaning? Their manager called. Fairly choking, he was. He said they could never take responsibility for such priceless carpets. He said we should have told him what they were before they picked them up. He said if we couldn't prove they were heavily insured and—what did he say?—that our insurance policy extended to cover him, he was going to deliver the carpets back to us by five o'clock tonight. Uncleaned. How do you like them green apples, Ambassador? I was about to call you about it."

"I don't know. . . ." he said absently. Without intending to, Mrs. Brown was giving him time to think. He was not thinking well.

"What am I to do about the carpets, Mr. Ambassador?"

"I don't know."

"Well, they'll deliver them back—"

"Fine," he said. "Right."

"Mr. Ambassador, there's nothing wrong, is there?"

"Absolutely not."

"Toby wasn't sick on the plane, or anything? All he had at the airport was orange juice."

"Everything's fine, Mrs. Brown. I expect I'll be in at my usual time."

"Should I try to call Mrs. Rinaldi in California about the carpets?"

"No," the Ambassador said. "Mrs. Rinaldi will be out of touch most of the afternoon."

He pushed the flashing button to extension 351.

"Christina?"

"Teddy? I'm a little worried."

He looked around the office at his staff. Each was quietly reviewing notes on United Nations Resolution 1176R—the culmination of years of intense diplomatic effort and, finally, negotiation; His Majesty's sole object of desire; a few words, really, that would do more than warships and tanks and planes to keep the Persian Gulf open for the flow of oil to the free world. They were only pretending not to hear his conversation.

Slowly, the Ambassador said to his wife, "I understand."

She said, "You mean there is reason to be worried?"

"Listen, Christina, I suggest you do the obvious, simple things." He had learned the wisdom of keeping people busy in a crisis. "Look around the airport, especially the baggage areas, the snack bars."

She said, "Yes."

"Have Brandt Airlines page Toby. That's simple. The kid knows his own name."

"Teddy, Mr. Svenson said Toby wasn't aboard that airplane. His reservation had been canceled."

He said, "I understand."

"Oh, my God! Teddy!"

Quietly, he said, "That's right."

"Oh, God!"

"Call me back in an hour or so," he said. "I won't leave the office."

He hung up and pushed the intercom button. "Sylvia, call Brandt Airlines and see if that plane Toby was on to California was a through flight. Make sure it didn't stop in Chicago, or wherever."

"It was scheduled as a through flight, Mr. Ambassador. That's why we put Toby on it."

"I see. Nevertheless, make sure the plane didn't land anywhere between here and San Francisco."

"Yes, sir."

The Ambassador sat back in his swivel chair and smiled blankly at his staff.

"Mrs. Brown seems to be having a domestic crisis," he said slowly. "Something about carpets. Getting carpets cleaned."

He blinked at their stares.

"Nevertheless, I think I shall suspend this conference for the moment. . . ."

The three staff members obediently put their papers in order and stood up.

"His Majesty's carpets may seem a small matter next to Resolution 1176R, but they are national treasures."

The Ambassador knew his dissembling was being ignored.

Ria Marti came to his desk and waited until the others had left the office.

She said, "Toby isn't missing, is he?"

He said, "This is about carpets, Ria. Embassy carpets."

"Mr. Ambassador." Ria was scrupulous about using his title in the Embassy offices and almost always at the Residence. "If this is about Toby, you've got to keep me informed from the very beginning. The press would be the hounds of hell on a matter of this sort."

Ambassador Teodoro Rinaldi smiled the smile that he knew had won more negotiations for him than all His Majesty's faith and power.

"Ria," he said, "skies may crumble and mountains tumble, but our young friend Toby will let nothing stand in the way of his trip to Fantazyland."

He saw that using his smile on her had convinced her that something was wrong.

As she was leaving the office, Sylvia's voice came over the intercom. "Mr. Ambassador, I've called Brandt Airlines. They have confirmed their Flight 203 today did not make a stop between New York and San Francisco. The plane landed at San Francisco International a few minutes ahead of schedule."

"Thank you." He kept his finger on the button. "Sylvia, get me His Majesty on the scrambler phone as quickly as possible. This is an emergency."

Two

Christina put her wallet, which had been open to her telephone credit card, into her purse and walked through the cavernous reception hall to the down escalator. In the baggage area, there were three carousels working. Slowly, she walked around each, peering into the crowds.

"Pardon me," she said to a man with an official-looking cap. "Could you tell me if the luggage from the Brandt New York Flight 203 has been picked up?"

The man looked at a wall clock. "That was carousel five. That's long gone, miss."

"Can you tell me if there was any baggage left unclaimed from that flight?"

"I can tell you there wasn't. Only flight we've had today, miss, with unclaimed luggage was from Mexico City. And people from the Bureau of Narcotics picked that up."

"I see. You're sure?"

Looking up over his shoulder, her eyes grew wide. "He's there! On the escalator!"

She sprinted. She jumped the first two steps of the escalator.

"Oh, please," she said to the people on the escalator as she tried to push through them.

"We're all in a hurry, you know," snapped a man with thick glasses.

"My son."

At the top of the escalator, she looked around the airlines' reception area.

A bell rang through the public-address system to gain attention for an announcement.

She turned.

"Toby!"

His hand was in that of a middle-aged woman who was leading him through glass doors to a parking area.

"Toby!"

She ran through the crowd to him.

Her arm hit the slow-moving automatic door. "Toby, Toby!"

She spun him around by his shoulders.

The child looked terrified.

"Hey!" The middle-aged woman jerked the boy's hand. "Who are you?"

"Oh, I'm sorry!" Christina said. "I'm sorry, I'm sorry."

The woman's pale blue eyes narrowed. "You need help, miss?"

"I'm sorry," Christina said. "My son—wasn't on his plane. I thought . . ."

The woman said, "I see. It's all right, Peter. The lady didn't mean to frighten you. Peter's my grandson," she said to Christina.

The woman was in pink slacks.

"Yes. I see. I'm sorry, Peter."

"Come on, Peter," the woman said. "We both missed our naps."

They went to the right, along the sidewalk. The boy looked back at Christina.

"I'm sorry," Christina said.

"I'm sorry." She sobbed. "I'm sorry."

Three

"My son appears to be missing."

Ambassador Teodoro Rinaldi had been told His Majesty, the King, was aboard the royal yacht, The Lioness, in the Persian Gulf. Using ship-to-shore, the scrambler system, and trans-world telephone, the Ambassador knew there would be long pauses between their comments to each other and that the King's well-modulated masculine voice would sound like that of Bugs Bunny. A rather slow Bugs Bunny.

"Was he abducted?" the King asked.

"We have no information at this time," the Ambassador said. "We only know that someone interfered in his affairs. Some third, unknown party canceled an airplane reservation in his name. Our housekeeper brought him to the plane. When the plane landed he was to be met by his mother, but he was not aboard the plane."

"Where was he going?"

"From New York to San Francisco," the Ambassador said.

"Why is Christina in San Francisco?" the King asked.

The Ambassador considered the King's ability to cut directly to the heart of a matter. He dreaded it.

"Vacationing. Tennis camp."

The answer seemed inconsequential.

"Why was Toby joining her on the West Coast?"

"Fantazyland. They were going to Fantazyland."

Through his United Nations office window New York had misted. The Ambassador blinked.

"Teddy," the King said. "Are things all right between you and Christina?"

"Yes, sir. She was just run-down and tired. Our efforts have been particularly constant, sustained, lately."

He stopped himself. Belatedly, his diplomatic training told him that the question would have been more convincingly answered with a single word. "Yes." Or "definitely." Or "absolutely."

The King would have realized—as the Ambassador had realized, sitting alone in his office waiting for his call to reach the King—that this was a particularly bad time to have his family away from the protection of the Embassy. He had been unwise—mistaken—in permitting it.

"Teddy. Do you believe Toby has been kidnapped?"

The Ambassador cleared his throat. "We know someone has interfered in his plans. At the moment, we do not know where Toby is. At the risk of causing you pain and anxiety needlessly," the Ambassador said, "I thought it would be best to let you know immediately."

"Teddy, I'm very sorry."

There was no question in the Ambassador's mind that the King's words were sincerely meant.

The King's grandfather had been a merchant. Simply that. A businessman.

A very successful businessman who had gathered unto himself almost every profit-making venture within his reach—banking, agriculture, shipping, oil—as a fat man finishes a bowl of olives put before him, almost not knowing he is doing it. In Italy and Switzerland and Europe at large, Teodoro Rinaldi's great-grandfather had been his contact man, his representative, his interpreter, his doer.

During World War I, the merchant bought himself a uniform (delivered from Switzerland by Rinaldi's great-grandfather) and set out to protect his various business interests in the Persian Gulf. Before the end of World War I, the Allies (persuaded by Rinaldi's great-grandfather) had decided it was in their best interest to draw a line around the merchant-general's various business interests and declare it a friendly nation.

Thus the merchant-general became a King.

And thus the Rinaldi family, originally Italian, subsequently Swiss, became loyal subjects of the King.

The present King, sixteen years older than Teodoro Rinaldi, was a brilliant, handsome man, carefully educated, at Oxford, the Sorbonne, the London School of Economics, to rule.

And Teodoro Rinaldi had been carefully educated, at Harvard College and Georgetown University, to serve his King in the family tradition as foreign representative.

Like few men in the twentieth century, neither considered that life had offered him an alternative.

"Have you informed anyone else that Toby may have been abducted?" the King asked.

"No, sir."

"I assume we're both thinking the same thing," the King said.

"Yes, sir."

"Resolution 1176R."

"Yes."

"But you've had no direct communication from the opposition that they mean to use your son's life as a weapon against you?"

"No, sir."

"You were right to tell me so quickly, Teddy."

"Thank you, Your Highness."

"It's conceivable you will have no direct communication. They might trust you to understand implicitly."

"Yes."

"Sabotage the Resolution or you lose your son."

The Ambassador did not answer.

The King said, "I will have my chief of American Intelligence at the Embassy within the hour."

"Mustafa? Do you mean Mustafa?"

"His name is Turnbull."

"I see." The Ambassador realized he should have known—he should have always realized—that Mustafa, the Embassy's chief of Intelligence—the nice little man with a mustache, very good at reading economic reports and breaking them down to facts relevant to the King, not very good at directing bodyguards, Embassy servants and staff—was not His Majesty's actual chief of Intelligence in the United States.

Before this, the Ambassador had never heard of Turnbull.

Again, he said, "I see."

"He's English trained," the King said. "Been in the United States a long time. You may have complete confidence in him."

"Yes, sir."

"Teddy," the King said, "we will stand together on this?"

It was a question.

Teodoro Rinaldi thought of the King standing over Toby's bassinet the very night he was born. Putting Toby on a polo pony at the age of three. Reading Uncle Whimsy comics to him during long flights in the royal jet. Playing with Toby in the snow at Gstaad.

But he was not Toby's father.

The Ambassador to the United Nations said to the King: "Yes."

*

"Mr. Ambassador?" Sylvia said. Mrs. Rinaldi's on 352."

"Thank you." Since talking with the King, Teodoro Rinaldi had sat back from his desk, hands in his lap, motionless, staring at his wastebasket.

"Christina? Any luck?"

"Teddy, I'm scared out of my mind."

Her voice was dry, her tone a little higher than natural, her throat tight.

"Are you still at the airport?"

"Yes."

"What have you done?"

"Everything I can think of. Searched all over this place. Snack bars. Restaurants. Parking lots. Had Toby paged. Checked with the V.I.P. lounge again. Checked Mr. Swenson. There is no unclaimed luggage from that flight."

"Christina, we don't know any more than we did an hour ago."

"Oh." Her voice sounded crushed. It was clear she hadn't been daring to ask. "Have you talked to the boss?"

"The boss" was their name for the King. It came from a ridiculous statement Teddy once made: "I work for a boss like any other boss." The King was not like any other boss. He was a monarch. A dictator. A man with absolute, life-and-death power over his subjects. A power he had never hesitated to use.

"Yes," the Ambassador said. "He sends you his greatest sympathy."

"Stuff that," the wife of the Ambassador said. "What's he doing for us?"

"Sending in the troops."

"What?"

"I'm going back to the Residence right now for a meeting with his top intelligence people."

"Not Mustafa. Oh, my God. Not that nice, little useless man."

"No. Not Mustafa."

"What shall I do? Teddy, I just can't believe Toby is in this airport, or ever was. His reservation was canceled."

"I know."

"Shall I come home? I think I should."

"No. Where does Toby expect you to be?"

"At the airport."

"No. I mean, where does that little packet Mrs. Brown made up for the airlines say you're staying? What was the contact number she gave for you?"

"The tennis camp's. I gave the tennis camp number."

"Then I suggest you go back to the tennis camp. Someone—even Toby—might have tried to call you there."

Then he realized he was giving her reason for false hope. A hope which would doubtlessly be dashed within the hour when she returned to the camp and learned there had been no calls. Her panic, her fear, would begin again.

"But, Teddy, this was my last day there. I'm all packed. Toby and I were going to spend the night in a motel on our way to Fantazyland."

"Does he or anyone else have the telephone number of that motel? I mean, was it listed in the information packet?"

"No."

"Then return to the tennis camp."

"I've checked out. My room is gone."

"I'm sure they can accommodate you somehow. But, Christina—?"

"Yes?"

"For now, tell no one what is going on."

She was silent.

"I mean, don't tell the police. Don't tell the people at the tennis camp."

"I've already told the people at the airlines."

"Don't worry. They won't be the ones to tell either the police or the press. Bad public relations for them. Unless they hear from you again, they'll be quick to assume the problem is solved."

"All right."

"We don't need more pressure on us at this point."

"No," she said, "we don't."

"I suspect there'll be someone out there talking to you before midnight, your time. Someone from our Intelligence Section."

"I don't have anything to tell them. Except that I'm scared to death, Teddy."

"I know. They should be able to help you. You want a doctor? Sedatives? Anything?"

"No," she said quickly. "I want Toby."

"Believe me, Christina, the best brains in the world will be on this. Immediately. You know the boss."

"Yes," she said. "I do. Teddy, there will be no problem about the ransom, will there?"

The question startled him. Ransom. Christina thought Toby had been kidnapped for ransom. An American girl. He had married a young American woman. For nine years she had been the wife of the Ambassador, but she had never really known what that had meant. Constant social engagements. Boring dinners. Quiet talks. Anger at him for staying up late. Not taking vacations. Being nice to people neither of them could stand. Toby had been kidnapped and she had presumed immediately he had been kidnapped for ransom.

It was highly unlikely she was correct.

"Of course not," he answered. "No problem."

"Even if it's millions and millions?"

"The boss will provide."

"I mean, he wouldn't stand back on some damned royal principle, would he?"

She stressed "royal" sardonically. Christina did not

think well of the two thousand, five hundred years of fictitious royal lineage the merchant-general-king's descendants had created for themselves. Another example of Christina's inability to understand the nature of power.

"Ransom will be no problem," Teddy said. He was certain the problem of ransom would never arise. Toby was kidnapped for reasons far greater than money.

"Christina? Go back to the tennis camp. We have the number there. I'm sure someone will come to you before midnight. Again, I repeat: tell no one about Toby."

"I won't."

"You'll just have to take this by yourself."

"I understand."

"Trust no one."

"Okay." There was annoyance in her voice.

"Christina, believe me. The longer we keep this quiet, the greater the chance Toby has of surviving."

"Oh, Teddy."

"Sorry, Christina. I had to say that."

Four

"Ambassador Rinaldi, let me get one or two things straight." Turnbull sat forward in the library chair, right forearm resting on his thigh, head angled aggressively toward the Ambassador.

"Your son was traveling alone?"

"Yes."

"And your wife is also traveling alone, on the West Coast?"

"Yes."

The Ambassador stared at His Majesty's chief of Intelligence in the United States. What should he say? That his wife and son were distinctly American in attitudes and found traveling with bodyguards cumbersome and embarrassing? That they all felt that bodyguards only increased the danger to them by drawing attention to them? That they had learned from experience that whatever arrangements the Embassy's Intelligence chief, the benighted Mustafa, made for them would just collapse anyway, causing a great confusion and greater complications?

The Ambassador said, "Let me make this straight to you, Mr. Turnbull—"

"Colonel Turnbull."

Teddy Rinaldi decided to ignore the title, for the moment.

"I am the highest-ranking representative of our nation in this country. I will not accept criticism, personal or professional, from you."

"Admit it, now, Ambassador Rinaldi. You made a mistake."

The Ambassador shrugged. How could he admit that his young American wife finally had rebelled against the tight strictures of Embassy life? Had insisted, reasonably, on getting away by herself for a while? Had insisted upon having a few happy days alone with her son, "play days," she called them, to take Toby to Fantazyland? How could he admit that he felt that if he hadn't agreed . . . he might have lost both his wife and his son? Immediately, the King had perceived all this: *Are things all right between you and Christina?*

"I might have made a more prudent decision," the Ambassador said slowly. "Fantazyland is not perceived as a threatening place."

He had let himself into the Residence—a fourteen-room condominium ten minutes' walk from the United Nations—with his own key and immediately found himself tripping over most of the Residence's carpets rolled up in the foyer. Mrs. Brown appeared, clucking about the carpets, and told him someone was waiting for him in the library.

The Ambassador had closed the library door behind him.

"You've gotten us into one fine mess." Turnbull scratched through his close-cropped, iron-gray hair vigorously enough to change the direction of whatever thoughts lay below the scalp. "Question is: how do I get us out of it?"

"We're talking about my son, Colonel."

"We're talking about Resolution 1176R," Turnbull snapped. "Mr. Ambassador."

"You know about Resolution 1176R?"

"Who do you think has done all the work on it?"

Calmly, the Ambassador said, "I think I have."

Colonel Turnbull glanced at him contemptuously.

The Ambassador had observed before that intelligence people were like crows: in announcing the portents of rain they think they are generating a storm.

"Tell me everything you know about this," Turnbull said, sitting back in his chair.

"First, Colonel Turnbull, tell me if you have sent someone to be with my wife."

"I'm going out myself," Turnbull snorted. "Now I want to know two things: what arrangements were made for your son, and who knew about them?"

"Would you like a drink, Colonel?"

"I would not."

"I thought it might be easier. . . ."

Muscles in his jaw flexing, notebook in his lap, pen in hand, Colonel Turnbull waited, saying nothing.

Teddy Rinaldi shrugged and began speaking in a calm, reasonable tone. "As I've said, Colonel, the pressures on my wife have been intense and long sustained. Very long. There has been a constant routine of meetings, lunches, cocktail receptions, dinners, day after day, including weekends, month after month, in our effort to educate other delegates and their governments regarding Resolution 1176R and attract their support and their votes—"

"You've been doin' your job, man. Get on with it."

"My wife was very tired. . . ." The Ambassador hesitated. ". . . Becoming a little nervous, irritable. You must remember that Christina is born and bred American."

Colonel Turnbull sighed, pointedly.

"There is this tennis camp in California, called The All-Stars', modestly enough, friends had recommended to Christina. She arranged to attend for ten days."

"Were the Embassy's intelligence staff notified of her plans?"

". . . Yes." *Poor* Mustafa.

"And no security arrangements were made for her?"

"None in particular, I believe. Embassy car to the airport, first-class flight, a hired limousine and driver meeting her in San Francisco—"

Colonel Turnbull shook his head.

"And your son, Toby?"

"Well . . . in fact, we haven't been able to see much of Toby lately. He attends boarding school in New Hampshire—"

"Eustace Academy."

"That's right. We thought we'd have some time this last summer, either at the beginning or the end of it, but Resolution 1176R has prevented our even taking a weekend. Toby was at that sailing camp on the Cape. Of course, we did take him to Gstaad for a few days with His Majesty last winter."

"Mr. Ambassador, I'm not looking for diplomatic phrasing. I'm looking for facts."

"All I'm trying to say is that my wife's desire—you might say, demand—to have some play days with our son, Toby, was entirely normal and correct."

"You're trying to excuse yourself for sending your wife and child off, at this point, with absolutely no security."

The Ambassador said, "I suppose I am."

"Give me your son's travel schedule."

"Yesterday afternoon he was driven by school staff to the airport in Boston and put aboard a plane for New York. Mrs. Brown met him at the airport and brought him to the Residence in the Embassy car."

"He spent overnight here at the Residence?"

"Yes."

"Did you see him?"

The Ambassador swallowed hard. "I had a meeting with the French delegation about the Resolution that went on until one thirty in the morning. I was at my desk at the Embassy at seven fifteen in the morning."

"Mr. Ambassador, how many months has it been since you've actually seen your son?"

"I looked in upon him the other night. When he was asleep."

"He was put aboard Brandt Airlines Flight 203 to San Francisco today?"

"Yes. It was a through flight."

"Who saw him off?"

"Mrs. Brown, our housekeeper. She took him to the airport in the Embassy car and turned him over to airlines personnel."

" 'Turned him over'?"

"Yes. You know how the airlines do these things. Putting a child alone on an airplane is rather like sending off a package. They get name tags stuck on them and packets full of names and addresses. It's all quite safe."

"Usually," said Colonel Turnbull. "Usually."

"My wife was to meet him at the San Francisco airport at about four o'clock. She was there in plenty of time, but . . . no Toby."

The Ambassador paused a moment. He knew his voice was about to crack.

Finally, he said, "My wife immediately appealed to airlines personnel for help in locating Toby. Here's a fact for you, Colonel Turnbull: the airlines manager in San Francisco told Christina that Toby's reservation had been canceled. In New York, the night before."

"What?" The Ambassador thought he'd let Turnbull put his mind around that hard fact himself. "What did you say?"

"Toby's reservation was canceled. And not by my office."

"Then Toby is still in New York?"

The Ambassador raised his hands. "Toby could be anywhere."

"Who made the travel arrangements for your son?"

"The Embassy. Overseen by my secretary, Sylvia Menninges."

"Did the Embassy Intelligence Section know about your son's travel plans?"

"Of course."

"Who else knew?" asked Colonel Turnbull.

"The travel agency—"

"What travel agency?"

"We always use the Mideast Airlines office here in New York for any family or Embassy traveling. We're obliged to. They make all the arrangements."

"So, doubtlessly, there were Embassy stickers all over the tickets. . . ."

"I suppose so."

"Therefore an unknown number of airlines personnel also knew that the Ambassador's eight-year-old son was skittering off to Fantazyland?"

The Ambassador's eyes ran along the top shelf of books across the room. "Skittering." Colonel Turnbull made it all seem very irresponsible.

He said, "My wife and son were taking a vacation. This was not an official trip."

The fat man flopped his hand impatiently.

"Who's this Mrs. Brown?"

"Our housekeeper."

"How long has she been with you?"

"Almost nine years. Since just before Toby was born, when we were stationed in London. She's sort of doubled as a nurse."

"Is she the woman who opened the door to me?"

"I suppose so."

"Is she a British citizen?"

"I think she's taken the opportunity to become an American citizen."

"I see. What other household staff is there?"

"Two drivers—"

"You mean, chauffeurs."

"Yes."

"Are they both American?"

"No. One is a Jamaican. The other is an American. From Brooklyn."

"Anyone else?"

"There's the cook."

"American?"

The Ambassador shook his head. "French. The houseman, who doubles as my valet—Pav—is a loyal subject. I've known him since we were boys."

The Colonel was shaking his head sadly.

"Are there complete intelligence dossiers on each of these people?"

"I trust so. You'd have to ask Major Mustafa."

"I will. Please ask this Mrs. Brown to come in. I want to question her."

As Ambassador Teodoro Rinaldi walked across the library to summon Mrs. Brown, he felt his legs hard with tension and already heavy from exhaustion.

Five

"Mrs. Brown, are you an American citizen?"

"I am, sir. Naturalized."

She sat on the edge of the library chair facing Colonel Turnbull, glancing nervously sideways at Ambassador Rinaldi.

"Toby," Colonel Turnbull said. "You picked him up at the airport yesterday at what time?"

"Oh, my God!" Her hand flew to her mouth. "Toby!" As she looked at the Ambassador, her sky-blue eyes seemed to shatter like glass. "Something's happened to Toby!"

"Mrs. Brown—" the Ambassador began.

"If you please, Ambassador," Colonel Turnbull said sternly.

"I do please," said the Ambassador firmly. "Mrs. Brown has been a member of this family since before Toby was born."

"I'd rather she had no information before I question her!"

Mrs. Brown, frightened eyes brimming with tears, was taking short gasps of air. "Toby?"

The Ambassador turned to the little, gray-haired woman in the big leather chair. "Mrs. Brown, I'm sure all this is just a false alarm . . . we're just being extra cautious. Toby seems to be missing. . . ."

"Missing?"

The Ambassador could only guess at what she was imagining. . . .

"This is Colonel Turnbull, sent here by His Majesty to help us."

She looked untrustingly at the Colonel. "I've never seen him before in my life."

The Ambassador smiled. "Neither have I, Mrs. Brown. Neither have I."

"Call the police," she blurted. "Call the New York police. Call the F.B.I."

"We can't do that. The Colonel is here to help us. If you'd just tell him everything you know. . . ."

Mrs. Brown found a handkerchief in her pocket and brought it to her face. She would be a good soldier. She would rise to the demand. She always had.

Colonel Turnbull said, "Mrs. Brown, what time did you pick Toby up at the airport yesterday?"

"Does Mrs. Rinaldi know?" she asked the Ambassador with renewed sharpness. "I mean, that Toby is lost?"

"Yes."

To her hands in her lap, to herself, she muttered, "Poor Christina."

"What time did you pick Toby up at the airport yesterday?"

"Five thirty."

"Was he on the Eastern Airlines shuttle flight from Boston?"

"Of course not. American Airlines. First class."

"Arriving in New York at five thirty?"

"The plane was due at five ten. It arrived a little before five thirty. At LaGuardia Airport."

"Where, precisely, in the airport did you meet Toby?"

"At the security gate. I had to wait outside. Only ticketed passengers are allowed through the security gate, the sign said."

Colonel Turnbull's eyes flickered at her. A sensible woman: one who obeyed signs. He said, "Was Toby alone when you found him?"

"I didn't 'find' him. He wasn't lost." Her eyes were wet. "At that point, anyway. He came walkin' down the corridor like the darlin' little man he is, grinnin' at me, his suitcase bangin' against his knee every step."

"Was he alone?"

"No, sir. There was a stewardess with him. From off the plane. They were quite chummy. She even bent and kissed him good-bye."

"The stewardess left you immediately?"

"Yes, sir."

"Then what did you and Toby do?"

"We went straight to the car."

"You didn't have to stop for baggage?" .

"Toby had his bag. Didn't I already say that? The poor lad didn't have all that much to carry."

"Where was the car?"

"It was in the taxi area. Double parked. DPL license plates, you know. Max didn't even open the trunk. He took Toby's bag in the front seat and we jumped in the back."

"Max?"

"Our driver," the Ambassador said. "One of our drivers."

"Mrs. Brown, while waiting at the airport, and after picking up Toby, going through the airport with him, were you aware of anyone watching you or following you?"

"Good heavens, no, sir. Then again, I'm not one to see evil lurking behind every bush."

"Then you shouldn't be working for an embassy," muttered the Colonel. "At least, not this Embassy."

"Of course, goin' through the airport with Toby, some people looked at him and smiled. People do that with Toby. He's such a beguilin' child."

Mrs. Brown blew her nose.

"Mrs. Brown," the Ambassador said gently.

Colonel Turnbull rolled on his hams. "What did you and Toby talk about?"

"You mean in the car?"

"At the airport, in the car, at the Residence. . . ."

"Well. First he told me about the stewardess. How he found out so much about her in an hour's flight, I'll never know."

"What was her name?"

"Ms. Gunn."

"One N or two N's?"

"How would I know?"

"What did he say about her?"

"He said she wasn't too shabby."

"' Wasn't too shabby'? What does that mean?"

"I think it means that he thought her beautiful."

"Oh."

"Her father was a doctor in Mississippi. She had a boyfriend in Atlanta, Georgia. The plane was going there next, and she would have dinner with him. His name was Jim."

"Did you understand from this that Ms. Gunn, the stewardess, was going back to the airplane and continuing her flight to Atlanta, Georgia, last night?"

"Yes, sir."

"Do you have any idea what Toby told her about himself?"

Mrs. Brown's eyebrows creased. "No, sir. Not at all."

"What else did Toby talk about?"

"He congratulated me on bein' pasteurized, the darlin'."

"' Pasteurized'?"

Mrs. Brown smiled. "He called me a 'pasteurized United States citizen.'"

"I still don't get it," Colonel Turnbull said. "Mrs. Brown, will you please speak English?"

Quietly, the Ambassador said, "Pasteurized: naturalized."

"I had been writin' him about my becoming a naturalized United States citizen," Mrs. Brown said. "So he congratulated me on becomin' pasteurized."

Colonel Turnbull shook his head. "What else did you and Toby talk about?"

"The trip to Fantazyland with his mother. He kept askin' me what I really thought it was like."

"What did you tell him?"

"I told him I'd never had the pleasure of bein' there."

"How much time did you spend with Toby last night, Mrs. Brown?"

"Well, we had supper together, in the kitchen, I went in on him while he was tubbin', and then talked with him for a while before he went to sleep."

"Mrs. Brown, was he in your opinion a well child?"

"'Well'?" Her eyes popped wide. "You never saw a handsomer, healthier child. Eight years old and not a speck of baby fat on him. His skin and his eyes and his hair just shine with health."

"Did he seem worried about anything? School? Work? Sports?"

"At supper he told me about his teachers and all his courses, and that he was the fastest runner in his class, beat everybody at the hundred-yard dash and made a record for his age running around the quadrangle in under three minutes. A very happy child, Colonel Turnbull."

"Neither you nor he left the Residence once you came home from the airport, and you did come straight here, no stops?"

"We made no stops, and neither of us left the Residence last night, or this morning, for that matter, until it was time for the car to take us to the airport."

"Was it the same driver who took you?" The Colonel looked at his notes. "This man you identified earlier as Max?"

"Yes. It's usually Max on duty during the daytime."

"Do you know this Max person well, Mrs. Brown?"

"As I say, Colonel, he's usually the driver on duty during the days. So he's usually the one who takes me shopping. He comes to the kitchen for coffee if he has to wait for the Ambassador or Mrs. Rinaldi, or soup and sandwich if he's ferrying people in and out for a luncheon party."

"You're a widow, Mrs. Brown?"

"That has nothing to do with Max. Max lives in Brooklyn with his wife of twenty-six years and the three of his five children who still live at home."

"Was there a Mr. Brown?"

"Of course there was."

"What happened to him?"

"He was run over by a bus. Twelve years ago. On the Kingsland Road. A good man, you may be sure, but not one noted for his sobriety."

"All right, now. Mrs. Brown." The Colonel's tone gentled. "I want you to tell me about taking Toby to the airport earlier today. Everything you can think of. Especially whether—at any point—you noticed anyone watching you and Toby. Whether you remember seeing any person—no matter what he or she looked like—more than once."

"It went as smooth as canned applesauce," Mrs. Brown said. "Max was waiting for us downstairs with the car. We went directly to the airport. I can hardly be expected to know if anyone was following us in a car. Wait a minute." Mrs. Brown frowned. "There was a funny vehicle that was in the lane next to us for a long time. Pulled up beside us at two or three red lights. Toby and I got a good look at it and laughed about it. It was a yellow van, with blue and red bugs painted all over it."

"Bugs?"

"The slogan written on the side was, *Get the bugs out.* Call Whatsis Termite Company."

"I see. Do you remember the name of the termite company?"

"No. I'd say it was a French name. Or Italian," she said hesitantly.

"This truck stayed with you a long time?"

"Two or three miles. But not 'with us.' More beside us. In the next lane."

"Did it go all the way to the airport with you?"

"No. I wouldn't say so."

"Did the driver of that truck show any curiosity regarding you and Toby? Did he look at you?"

"Of course. People are always curious about people riding in the back of a limousine. But the funny thing about that truck was that it had wiggly antennas just over the windscreen. . . ."

"You mean, radio antennae?"

"No," Mrs. Brown said decisively. "Bug antennas. Like bugs have. They wiggled as the truck moved along. Most comical, they were. Toby had never seen such a truck, no more'n I had."

"All right, Mrs. Brown. At the airport, what did you do?"

"Went to the Brandt Airlines ticket counter, waited only a few minutes. I did change queues. First queue I got into there was a man at the counter makin' a perfect nuisance of himself, something about his refusing to pay overweight charges on his luggage, a lot of camera equipment, I understood him to be talkin' about, so I went to the next queue and the man there was very friendly, smiled at Toby and with a straight face asked if he wanted to sit in the Smoking or the Non-Smoking section. Toby, being Toby, said he wanted to sit in the Pizza section.

"I told the airline's representative Toby was traveling alone, and I tried to show the man our ticket, I mean, Toby's ticket, and the packet of information the airlines people had given us, but after a minute or two talking to Toby the man said, 'Seeing you have a special person here, we're going to let you both go right through security down to the waiting area for Gate 18.' He said someone would meet us there and check us through so I could meet the stewardess or steward who would be on the plane with Toby, and I said—"

"Wait a minute, Mrs. Brown." Colonel Turnbull held up his hand. "Are you saying that the man at the airline's counter did not look at Toby's ticket?"

"No. He didn't. He understood this was a child traveling cross-country alone and special arrangements had been made for him."

"As far as you know, he did not even check to confirm Toby's reservation on that flight?"

"No. Why should he? We were there in plenty of time, and someone was going to do that 'specially for us at the gate."

"Did you give him Toby's name?"

"Not his whole name. I think the first thing I said was, 'This is Toby. He'll be traveling with you to San Francisco, Flight 203. Here's his travel packet. What do we do?'"

"And, although layin' his charm out for you and the boy, Mrs. Brown, in fact the airline's counter representative told you to wait until you got to the gate before checking in?"

"Yes. So I'd be sure to meet the stewardess." Mrs. Brown's cheeks turned pink. "I'm pretty sure the young man thought I was Toby's grandmother."

Colonel Turnbull said to the Ambassador, "The reservation was not confirmed."

The Ambassador said, "I see that."

Mrs. Brown looked worriedly from one to the other. "Did I do something wrong?"

Colonel Turnbull said, "No, Mrs. Brown. It's just

that we need to check Brandt Airlines' routine for children traveling alone."

The Ambassador said, "It would make sense to have children checked in at the boarding gate. It would make sure that they were accompanied by an adult to that point. And it would allow the adult to meet the flight's stewardess, to have personal contact with whoever would be with the child during the flight."

"Steward," said Mrs. Brown. "It was a steward. He was waiting for us. And he told me I couldn't go through security with Toby."

"Wait a minute, Mrs. Brown," Colonel Turnbull said.

"I'm just saying I never did go to Gate 18 with Toby. The airline's steward met us in the corridor. Just as we were comin' to security, this young man came up to us. He said, 'Is this Toby Rinaldi?' I said, 'Yes, he is. I'm Mrs. Brown. Are you the young man from the airline?' and he said he was."

"Did you get his name?"

"Of course I got his name. Willins."

"Willins?"

"Willins," said Mrs. Brown. "Two I's, two L's. I always make sure of names, especially if I'm handing Toby over to someone. He asked for Toby's ticket and his information packet, looked at them as well as he could, poor boy, said, 'That's okay,' then picked up Toby's bag and headed back toward the airline terminal with it. He told us to wait for him there."

"Mrs. Brown, did this person show you any credentials proving he was an airline's representative?"

"No, sir. I didn't ask."

"Then how do you know he was from the airline?"

"He was waiting for us. He knew Toby's name. He was wearing one of those blazers all the airlines' representatives wear. At least, the men do."

Colonel Turnbull sighed. "Can you describe this man Willins to us?"

"I didn't like him, at first. He wasn't tall, but he had very big shoulders and chest. At first, something about him struck me as untrustworthy, but then I saw one of his eyes was perfectly still. I guess it was glass."

Turnbull's head jerked up.

"He had a glass eye?"

"Yes, sir, I think so. And his face was rough and scratched. He had my sympathy, lookin' at him."

Colonel Turnbull hesitated. "What else did you and this Willins man say to each other?"

"He didn't say much. When he came back, Toby asked to have his name tag pinned on him. The man—Willins—didn't seem to care much about that, so I asked him if I could do it, and he said, 'Sure,' so I pinned it on Toby, makin' a kind of ceremony out of it."

The Colonel cut in. "Is there anything else you can think of that might help us, Mrs. Brown?"

"Why, no, sir. I don't think so." Agony was in her eyes.

"Just one more thing, Mrs. Brown: you didn't actually see Toby get aboard that airplane?"

"How could I have, sir? I was left way down the corridor. Last I saw of Toby was walkin' down that corridor beside the airline's representative."

"I see."

Mrs. Brown was crying quietly.

Colonel Turnbull said to the room at large, "I'd like to interview the rest of the staff."

Mrs. Brown said, "I'll get them, sir."

The two men watched Mrs. Brown walk across the bare floor to the library door.

The Ambassador asked, "You'll be joining my wife, Colonel?"

The Colonel looked at his watch. "I'll fly to the Coast immediately."

"That's good," the Ambassador said. "Someone should be with her."

Six

Closer to Baltimore than Washington, Simon Cord pulled off the highway into a McDonald's parking lot.

He held the door open for a family leaving the restaurant, a mother carrying one child while towing another along by hand, followed by a tired-looking husband putting his billfold back into his pocket. The man nodded his thanks at Cord.

At the side of the restaurant, Cord dialed the Rinaldi family's private number at the Residence in New York. At the instructions of the operator, he stuck a correct assortment of coins into the slot.

The phone answered on the first ring.

"Ambassador Rinaldi," Cord said.

"Speaking."

"You're Ambassador Rinaldi?"

"Yes. What is it?"

Cord was surprised the Ambassador answered his own phone, and on the first ring. That was good: he had already gotten the message.

"Mr. Ambassador, we have your son. Tobias."

Cord listened to the silence for a moment. Then he heard the Ambassador take a breath.

"Let there be no mistake about it, Mr. Ambassador. The people I work for do not want Resolution 1176R submitted to the United Nations."

"What have you to do with the closing of the Persian Gulf to the shipping of oil?" The Ambassador was expostulating, nearly blurting. "What has that to do with my son?"

"I don't know anything about that, Mr. Ambassador."

"What has it to do with you?"

"I don't know anything about it. All I know is what I'm told by the people I work for."

"Who do you work for?" The Ambassador was shouting. "Who's hired you?"

"I'm just hired to do a job—"

"What job?"

"Kidnap your son. We've done that."

"Brave! Some man you must be. Kidnap an eight-year-old child—"

"Man enough to murder him."

"What?"

"If you give that speech. If you submit Resolution 1176R to the United Nations, we'll kill your son. And we won't give him a nice death. Child or no. We'll make sure the body is found so you and your wife will see what your child went through before he died."

Cord listened. The Ambassador was breathing heavily.

The Ambassador said, "Bastard."

"Oh, I'm much worse than a bastard, Mr. Ambassador. Do you doubt it?"

". . . No."

"Listen: if you're having any problems with this—if you think we haven't got your kid, or if you think we won't kill him—would you like us to send you his ear, or a finger or something?"

"Where are you?" the Ambassador said.

"How about answering my question? You want to get your son's foot in the mail? We don't want you to have any doubt at all."

"I have no doubt," the Ambassador said.

"No doubt?"

"No."

"Okay. Just be a good boy, Mr. Ambassador, and do what you're supposed to do. No Resolution."

Cord hung up.

The restaurant was about half full. Every table

where people sat was littered with paper. There was more paper visible than food.

Cord walked down an aisle between the tables, toward the front door. A handbag was on the floor. He picked it up and handed it to an elderly woman eating a hamburger.

He smiled. "You might lose it," he said.

How nice of you," she said, taking it with her free hand. "There are still gentlemen in the world. . . ."

Seven

Going to the airport, Christina had been happier than she had been in a long time. She had had ten days of good exercise, tennis morning and afternoon, plenty of sunshine by the pool, healthy diet, early nights, good novels to read. Better than all that, for ten days she had been away from New York, away from the Embassy, away from Teddy, with his tired, drawn face, his long, diplomatic, involved answers to her most simple questions. Better than anything, relaxed, refreshed, she now got to spend a few days with her son, Toby, alone, together with him, exploring Fantazyland. She had felt fit to take on the world.

In recent months, no matter how she had tried to supress it, her discontent had been growing. *Nothing is ideal,* she had tried to assure herself. *No one is perfectly happy. What is that line? Every happily married woman is putting up with something she can't stand? Something like that. . . .*

Day in and day out, night after night, Christina realized she was putting up with more and more things she really couldn't stand. At breakfast every morning, gently, firmly, conversationally, Teddy, in fact, would give her her orders for the day: what invitations she was to accept, what invitations she was to send, what letters she was to write, what phone calls she was to make, what, in each case, she was to say and how she was to say it. He would tell her with whom she was to have lunch, and where, and what was to be said at lunch. In the afternoon, what members of the legation staff she was to see and how she was to handle them. Where dinner would be and at what time, roughly how she should dress, with whom she should make a

point of speaking, and again, what she should say—
always what she should say. And late at night, she and
Teddy would sit in their robes in their bedroom for
another half hour or hour, and again conversationally,
as if it weren't desperately important, Christina would
report to Teddy in detail everything she had seen,
heard or otherwise perceived during that day. Teddy
complimented her continually and referred to her as
"my eyes, my ears, my heart."

She had become better at her job as she had come
to know well most of the people with whom she had
to deal. She developed a subtlety at working around
evasive answers while answering evasively herself.
Sometimes she even saw the whole diplomatic process
as an amusing game: *You've got a fact, and I want it;
I've got a fact and you're not going to get it unless I
want you to have it.*

Odd things bothered her. At first, her facial muscles
literally hurt from smiling. Her feet and the small of
her back hurt from the constant cocktail parties and
receptions. She consulted a doctor, who told her that
standing still for prolonged periods was the most difficult and unnatural exercise the human body could
perform. She learned to find excuses for walking
across a room, up or down a flight of stairs, to the
ladies' room, to go sit next to someone for a five- or
six-minute chat. Whenever she could escape the legation, she would go for as much of a walk around New
York as time permitted. And even though she would
restrict herself to a single glass of wine at each func-
tion, every morning when she awoke there would be
the mild headache, the stale taste in her mouth—
complaints from sinuses and lungs that had consumed
too much of other people's cigar, pipe, cigarette
smoke and whiskey, gin and vodka fumes.

Her job. Her sensible mother had said that mar-
riage was *a job.* What she meant, of course, was the

job of being a wife, helpmate, mother, friend, sexual partner. . . . She did not mean the job of being a professional diplomat.

Christina Finch was born and raised in Flemmington, Pennsylvania, which in those days was shifting from a strictly agricultural area to a mixed suburban, rural community. Most of the farms were being given up. Two, redesigned to look like college compuses, had become headquarters for international corporations. One had been turned into a country club. Most had been turned into housing developments.

Her mother's family, the Reardons, owned most of the best farmland and, except for a few acres of road frontage here and there, had held onto it. Each of her three uncles still ran a sizable farm. Her father had put together his initially small country law practice with a real estate brokerage firm and an insurance agency and done very well. There was some grumbling among the established families of the town that Ol' Finch had made a fortune developing everybody's real estate but his wife's family's, which was left intact at ever-increasing values. But the town elected him mayor four terms running.

Christina's two older brothers had been the football and basketball stars of the town. One had gone on to West Point. The younger had taken his medical degree from the University of Pennsylvania and then surprised the world by becoming a minister.

Christina's own youth had been as ideal as possible. At school, although no mean basketball player herself, she led the cheerleading at her brother's more noted athletic events, absolutely secure in their protection of her. Summers she spent working around her uncles' farms, again absolutely secure in their protection. Being the mayor's daughter, Christina became an expert buffer, making peace between youngsters born in the town and those moving into it. She was vice-president of her sophomore class and president of her senior class.

She had had no difficulty adjusting to college in North Carolina. Knowing her home would always be waiting, she dreamed vague dreams of New York and London and Paris but had no real expectation of ever being part of that world.

Then some committee asked her to play hostess to this diplomat from the Middle East who was coming to Chapel Hill to give a lecture.

She was at the airport on time, looking for a man in flowing robes and thick dark glasses. No such man appeared.

Finally, a slim, handsome but slightly tired-looking man, dressed in blue corduroy trousers, came up to her and said, "Hey, are you from the college?"

"Yes."

"Here to pick up someone named Rinaldi?"

"Yes," she said. "Are you here to see him, too?"

"I'm Rinaldi," he said.

"My God!" she said. "You're a diplomat?"

Seeing her shock, he said, "I guess I'm not."

The hotel where he was to stay, being state owned and run, did not serve meals on Sunday, so Christina found herself spending more time with him than she expected. She discovered he loved roast beef sandwiches with mayonnaise and strawberry milk shakes. Sunday night he said he didn't particularly want to go back to the hotel and rest, so they saw a movie. They stopped by an off-campus eatery and had beer and pizza. He didn't say much about himself, and she was too mystified by him to ask. He did say he had gone to school in Switzerland and to college in the United States. He said he liked listening to The Who but liked Eric Clapton even better.

The next day at the lecture she saw him for the first time as a diplomat, dressed in a dark blue suit, white shirt and red tie. She thought his lecture brilliant. Members of the audience that she knew were there to boo ended up asking respectful questions.

At the airport, saying goodbye to her, he touched his lips to her cheek so easily, so briefly, she wasn't really aware he had kissed her until after he had left. She knew she had fallen in love with Teddy Rinaldi, but she told herself it was just a schoolgirl infatuation for a sophisticated older man.

Wednesday he called her and asked if she could spend the weekend with him in Washington. She said no, thought for forty-five minutes, called him back and yelled, "Yes!"

Shortly, she knew it was Teddy Rinaldi she loved, his children she wished to be her children. Over long dinners he would try to describe the world of diplomacy. Only vaguely did she realize he was trying to warn her. Dumbly, she kept nodding her head yes.

Diplomacy: hadn't she been the town peacemaker? President of her senior class? Hadn't her father been reelected three times as mayor of Flemmington, Pennsylvania?

When they were first married, stationed in London, there had been frequent trips, vacations, breaks from routine. There had been Teddy's business trips home, long weekends in Scotland or Wales, or an occasional week in Portugal, or on the King's yacht in the Mediterranean, or skiing as part of the entourage in Switzerland. Even after Teddy was assigned to the United Nations in New York, there had been summer weekends on Long Island or Martha's Vineyard, winter weekends in Stowe, and vacations in Saint Croix or the Laurentians. And she and Toby and Mrs. Brown had spent many happy weeks at Christina's home in Pennsylvania.

Since Resolution 1176R had been conceived by Teddy and the King, there had been no such breaks.

In fact, she could not remember a single quiet dinner alone with her husband in over a year. Once, when Teddy had flu, he spent three days in bed. He worked there, too, but at least for three days she felt she had some of his personal attention.

What was most wrong with present circumstances was that it never let up. Christina was never seeing Teddy except formally, professionally. She was never seeing Toby at all. She felt she was losing touch with herself. One night before she had left New York, Teddy, tired and discouraged, had told her that it might be months yet before he would be scheduled to submit Resolution 1176R to the United Nations. Some African emergency had arisen. Christina was no longer sure she believed in Resolution 1176R.

Despite what her life had become, regardless of how hard she tried at her job, she remained Christina Finch, from Flemmington, Pennsylvania. To the diplomatic community (and to Teddy, she knew) she was *only* the Ambassador's young American wife, bright, attractive, very nice, of course, but without the training, the background necessary for such a position.

During crisis circumstances, Christina was not considered. Suddenly, Ria Marti would appear at Teddy's left elbow. Ria would know what was going on. Ria would represent the legation at receptions and dinners. Christina would find herself waiting in the bedroom late at night while Teddy and Ria consulted in the legation's office, or at Ria's apartment. At four o'clock one morning when Teddy came in from Ria's apartment, Christina threw a framed photograph of Toby at him.

He had never mentioned the incident. He had understood. Diplomats always understood.

But the incident had happened.

Christina was a terrific asset during business as usual, but given a crisis, she was supposed to withdraw and leave matters in the hands of the professionals. And they had been living under crisis circumstances for an inhumanly long time.

She still loved Teddy, but flying out to California, alone, divorce had been very much on her mind. She could make a home for Toby in Flemmington, Pennsylvania, where he would be safe and would know he was loved. She could go back to being involved in the lives of the people in her town, people she knew and loved—real people.

After her ten days of tennis and sunlight and swimming at the All Stars' Tennis Camp, Christina felt much stronger. She had not dropped the idea of divorce or, at least, separation from Teddy. She could, though, admit she still loved him.

For the moment she had decided to spend as much time as possible with Toby and try to discover how he felt about the school in New Hampshire, about never seeing his parents, about being yanked about by one adult after another.

She believed her vacation with Toby was going to be the most crucial few days of her life.

*

In leaving the airport, Christina suffered an agony the likes of which she had never known nor thought possible. Her heart, her mind, her nerves could not accept the idea of Toby *kidnapped.*

She drove stiffly, her legs braced with tension, fingers tight on the wheel, tears rolling down her cheeks below her sunglasses.

Rested, relaxed, she had begun to think she could get on top of her problems.

Someone has taken Toby! . . . Toby! . . . My God, my God. . . . Someone has taken Toby. . . .

Eight

In his apartment in Washington, Cord came out of the bathroom and answered the bedside princess phone.

"Cord? Something's wrong."

Cord's answer was sharp, annoyed. "How could there be? The kid was snatched. I already spoke with the Ambassador. On that private number you gave me."

"He was snatched, but not by Dubrowski."

"Turnbull, what are you talking about?"

"The chap at the airport who picked up Tobias Rinaldi was not Dubrowski. The housekeeper's description doesn't fit. Dubrowski's a big, muscular, handsome guy. Mrs. Brown describes the airline representative who snatched the kid as short, heavy shouldered—"

"Descriptions people give are never accurate."

"—with a glass eye. She couldn't have been mistaken about that, Cord."

Cord sat on the edge of his bed. "Gus. . . ."

"What happened to Dubrowski, Cord?"

"I don't know."

"Did you give him any money in advance?"

"Yes. Some."

"How much?"

"Five thousand dollars."

"You gave five thousand dollars to a junkie?"

"He's been straight, Gus. Gone into the body-beautiful bit. I used him on that thing in Rome, the bomb—"

"Cord, right now we don't know where the kid is or who has him. Where's Dubrowski? Answer me that! Who is this other boyo who grabbed the kid?"

Simon Cord studied his white feet on the aquamarine rug. "I don't know, Gus."

"You bloody well better find out, Cord."

"I'll go to to New York—"

"I'm on my way to the West Coast. The kid's mother is out there, and the kid knows it. You find Dubrowski."

"I will, Gus. Don't agitate your fat."

❋

Simon Cord shaved as carefully as always.

When he had been called to the United Nations and given the assignment to kidnap the Rinaldi boy by the Nine Nation Coalition, by training he immediately had set about two tasks. The first was to get someone else to commit the actual crime, preferably a known criminal, an ex-convict, devoid of political interest, for an amount of money substantial enough so that when the time arrived to maim the boy, later to murder him, the tasks would be carried off without hesitation. Donald Dubrowski had served two sentences for robbery. Twice he had been indicted for but not convicted of murder. He had had a drug habit, but the last time he had left prison he was clean and determined to stay clean. Although a little past his prime for such a sport, he had put in between forty and fifty hours a week body-building. For ten thousand dollars, Cord had assigned him to blow up the car of an Italian banker in Rome. Dubrowski had done so, killing the banker, his driver, and a woman and child who had been waiting on the sidewalk for a bus. The assignment had not phased him even slightly. For this Rinaldi assignment Cord had agreed to pay Dubrowski fifty thousand dollars. He had given him five thousand in advance.

Cord's second immediate task had been to secure

someone in the Rinaldi household to cooperate with him, provide information about the family's travel plans, security arrangements, etc. This had proved remarkably easy. A decade before, he and Augustus Turnbull had known each other in Cairo. It was simple enough, as an old friend, to call up Turnbull and invite him to lunch. The representatives of the Nine Nation Coalition had identified Augustus Turnbull as His Majesty's chief of Secret Intelligence in the United States.

Like any two businessmen discussing a deal of some dimensions, they enjoyed a long lunch against one wall of the Four Seasons. Cord saw to it that Turnbull had plenty of gin. Gently, he sounded Turnbull out about the Rinaldi family. Turnbull's caginess dissipated with remarkable alacrity.

Turnbull's hatred for the Rinaldi family was personal, profound, obsessive, insane. Speaking of them, his face reddened, his hands shook. Cord was surprised to see Turnbull had gained so much weight in ten years. He did not seem to be in complete control of his emotions. Cord gave him a long, drinking afternoon and early evening. Turnbull fantasized they were back in Cairo and told Cord everything.

A few days later, they met again. Turnbull did not remember having told Cord so much. Cord remembered. He assured Turnbull he would spoil Turnbull's plans for the Rinaldi family if Turnbull did not cooperate with him. He also assured Turnbull that Turnbull's best way of implementing his own plans for the Rinaldi family was to work with Cord. Once they had completed this assignment successfully, Turnbull could destroy the Rinaldi family, individually and as savagely as he liked. Cord would help.

Turnbull, Turnbull, Turnbull. Cord wiped the lather off his face. He wondered if he had made two mistakes: Dubrowski and Turnbull.

Nine

"Have there been any calls for me?" The young woman behind the tennis camp's reception desk radiated untroubled health and happiness. "Christina Rinaldi. Has anyone called for me?"

"No, Mrs. Rinaldi. No calls."

"I mean, someone didn't call and you said I'd checked out, or anything?"

"No. I've been here at the switchboard since two o'clock."

Christina found herself leaning forward, ribs suddenly against the high reception desk.

"No calls for me . . . ?"

Concern flickered in the young woman's face. *She thinks I'm staggering drunk,* Christina realized.

"Listen," Christina said. "I have a problem. Something's come up. I have to have my room back."

"Your room?"

"Yes. I need to—I have to stay the night."

"I'm sorry, Mrs. Rinaldi." The girl looked at her chalk board. "We've given your room to a Mrs. Uhlmann, from Toronto. She's already arrived, I'm afraid."

"Some other room," Christina said. "You must have some other room available. Anything."

"No," the girl said. "This is our busy season. Every room is taken." Again she looked at her chalk board. "If you're having trouble with your travel arrangements, I could phone around and find a room for you in a motel until you get things straightened out—"

"No!" Christina's right hand was a tight fist on the reception desk. "I have to stay here! It's very important!" She knew she was speaking too loudly. People always speak too loudly when there are things they can't say. "Please," Christina said senselessly, "can't you help me?"

The young woman stared into Christina's eyes.

"Mrs. Rinaldi, are you all right?"

"Look," Christina said. "*Tell no one Toby is missing,*" Teddy had said. "Listen. This is the only telephone number my son has for me. If I'm not here . . ."

"Your son can't be very old," the girl commented.

"He isn't. He's just a little boy."

The girl looked at her chalk board again, hesitated.

"Please," Christina said.

"I suppose you could take a staff bungalow. Mark, one of our tennis pros, is away, playing in the C.R.A. tournament in Santa Barbara."

"Oh, yes. Please. Anything."

The young woman looked into Christina's eyes again, to confirm that something was seriously wrong, something she didn't understand. "We've never done this before. The bungalow's probably quite a mess. Twenty-five-year-old bachelor—God knows what you'll find. No housekeeping."

"That's marvelous," Christina said. "I really appreciate this."

"Hang on," the young woman said. "I'll get Mark's key. I'm sure he won't mind. I—I think it's upstairs in my jacket."

Ten

On the flight to San Francisco, Colonel Augustus Turnbull was assigned an aisle seat in the Non-Smoking, first-class section.

A man was sitting in the window seat.

When Turnbull opened the overhead locker to stow his own coat, the other man's coat and two packages fell out.

Turnbull dumped them in his lap.

"Why don't you go sit somewhere else?" Turnbull asked.

He slammed the locker hatch closed and fitted his girth to the wide seat. He then aimed a kick at the man's attaché case, under the chair in front of them. The man's case sprung open.

Turnbull turned slightly toward the man, folded his hands over his stomach and stared at him.

The man's eyes were roaming around the first-class section.

The stewardess leaned over them. "Is there a problem?"

"Nothing I can't solve," the man said.

Leaning over, he closed his attaché case and picked it up. Holding it and his coat and packages, he stood up. "I'm changing my seat, stewardess."

The stewardess glanced at Turnbull. "That's fine, sir. There are other seats available."

Turnbull snorted.

"Would you let the gentleman out, please, sir?"

Sighing, as if he were doing everyone a favor, Turnbull stood up and moved into the aisle. At the man's first step into the aisle, Turnbull pushed past him and squeezed into his own seat again.

He listened to the stewardess settling the man into a seat two rows behind him.

The stewardess then leaned over Turnbull again.

"Is there anything else I can do for you, sir?"

"Yes," Turnbull answered. "You can turn off that scratching music."

"The music, sir, is for the enjoyment of the other passengers."

"This passenger isn't enjoying it."

"Once airborne, sir, would you like me to bring you a glass of champagne?"

"Double bourbon for me."

"Yes, sir. Please fasten your safety belt. I'd hate to lose you, sir."

Turnbull leaned out to watch the muscles in the stewardess's calves as she walked up the aisle. He sighed. He pulled up the chair arm to his left and let himself expand wider in the seats.

Turnbull didn't know quite how he became so fat. One day he just noticed a pounding in his temples, a ringing in his ears, a shortness of breath and looked at himself.

He was covered with blubber.

His life had been active—physically very active. He had always been able to eat five square meals a day. It had always burned off in physical activity.

Once he became His Majesty's chief of Intelligence in the United States, his physical activity became negligible. He spent hours a day on the telephone directing his operatives, hours a day in cocktail lounges and restaurants, wining and dining government officials: members of Congress, the military, the various departments.

Again, Turnbull snorted. *That blithering idiot Rinaldi—Ambassador Teodoro Rinaldi—thinks he's done the work on Resolution 1176R.* Turnbull patted his stomach.

Colonel Augustus Turnbull knew the truth.

The music went off. They became airborne. The stewardess immediately brought him a plastic glass with ice cubes in it and two shot-bottles of bourbon.

Colonel Augustus Turnbull had had great difficulty even being in a room with Teodoro Rinaldi. Looking at him. Talking to him. Listening to him. Pretending to question him. Watching the man's servants march before him.

Turnbull realized it was a good thing he had played out the questioning. He had expected to know the answers. Impatiently, brusquely, he had interrogated the Ambassador, savoring his own superior knowledge and role in this affair. He had Rinaldi where he wanted him.

Mrs. Brown was speaking. Turnbull was not listening closely. What was she saying? What did the man at the airport look like? He asked for the man's description again.

It wasn't Dubrowski.

The Rinaldi child was really missing. . . .

Turnbull swallowed his double bourbon in one gulp. He slammed his chair back into a reclining position. He heard the woman behind him say, "Ouch! Hey. . . ." He put his head back against the cushion.

He'd have to be far more coy with Christina Rinaldi than he had been with the Ambassador. *To find the kitten, follow the cat.*

The bourbon sloshed in his stomach.

*

The man who rode in the Jeep. The small, white man with the mustache that was too big for his face. The plantation owner. A high government official. Very close to the King.

The boy, Augustus, knew this was only one of the rich man's plantations. Far from the capitol.

The owner visited the plantation only twice a year, once in the fall and once in the spring. He was driven around in his Jeep.

When he would pass by the small, dusty frame house where Augustus lived with his mother, she would watch the Jeep, watch him. Her face would be totally expressionless.

The rich man in the Jeep would never wave or look her way.

When the rich man came to their house after dark, he always drove the Jeep himself. There was never anyone with him.

There had been other children in the Turnbull family, but they were so much older Augustus had only a dim impression of them. One son went to work on a neighboring plantation and was never heard from again. Another joined His Majesty's Army. Turnbull discovered later he had been beaten to death in a barracks fight. Still later he heard a whorehouse in Mosul, Iraq, was run by a woman named Turnbull, and Augustus wondered if she were his half sister. He never went to that whorehouse.

The senior Turnbull had been the overseer of the rich man's plantation.

Augustus had heard the story of his death many times. It had happened two or three years before he was born.

Turnbull had fallen into a threshing machine.

The workers brought him back to the house in a wagon dragged by a mule, but by the time they got him there he had bled to death.

His mother told him many times of her looking into the back of the wagon. Her husband's body was so bloody and mangled she had difficulty understanding what it was.

She always spoke of the flies. Her husband's body was black with flies.

Augustus and his mother lived alone in the house—except for the nights the owner was there.

The man who rode in the Jeep. The small, white man with the mustache that was too big for his face.

The man who rode his mother.

Rinaldi.

"Augustus! Come here! Come here this instant!!"

He was eight years old. Just the age, now, of Teodoro Rinaldi's son.

"Augustus!! Here!"

It was his mother calling.

When the owner came to the house in the Jeep after dark, Augustus always stayed in the back of the house. Sometimes there was yelling, sometimes laughter.

Tonight there had been yelling.

The kerosene light in the front room was hard on his eyes.

His mother's nightdress had been torn. Her left breast hung out. The nipple looked red, inflamed.

Rinaldi stood near the upright piano. There was something wrong with his eyes. They were watery, red. He was swaying.

"Your son, Rinaldi," his mother said.

Rinaldi said, "So what?"

"So don't think I can't get myself to the capitol."

Rinaldi put his hand on top of the piano, lowered his forehead onto his wrist. "You'd be shot before you were ten miles from here. Who cares anyway? Who'd believe you?"

His mother said, "Everyone."

"Who cares?" Rinaldi asked again.

"You have another son now. Your official son. Little Teodoro. Your wife."

"Shut up."

"You promised a lot, Rinaldi, Enough money to live on. Luther died working for you."

"He fell in the threshing machine. He was drunk."

"You're sober?"

"I'm not working a threshing machine."

"You said proper education for the boy—for Augustus—a proper education."

Rinaldi raised his head. He was sweating. It took him a moment to refocus his eyes.

"What do you want?"

"Money to go to England. I can't stand this heat anymore. The food. The flies. I'm old, Rinaldi, now. I'm thirty-nine. I look like I'm in my fifties. The heat, the sun. The flies. Just money. Just to go to England. That's all I want now."

"You'd never adjust."

"I can't live here anymore. I can't stand it. The isolation. I've given you enough. You've got to let me go!"

Rinaldi focused on Augustus.

"Yes," she said. "School! School for the boy."

Rinaldi came across the room. Passing Augustus, he didn't even stop.

The back of his hand smashed into Augustus's face.

The side of Augustus's head hit the wall. He found himself sitting on the floor next to the wall.

"Little bastard," Rinaldi said.

Augustus remained on the floor. He heard the Jeep start and immediately gun down the road.

"It's all right," his mother said. "He'll do something now."

They arrived in Liverpool, England, in November, when Augustus was eight years old. His mother never did adjust. She worked in a factory, joined a church and went to a neighborhood pub on Saturday nights.

When Augustus was twelve years old, he came home from school on a January Monday to find his mother hanging by her neck from a pipe in the kitchen. For him, then, it was institutions until he was old enough to be put into the Army.

He served two hitches, then spent eight years in various African nations as a mercenary. Finally he returned to England and rejoined the British Army with the understanding he would be assigned to Army Intelligence. Of course, after full training, he was assigned to the Persian Gulf States.

It was while he was recovering from a three-day drunk in a fleabag hotel in Sirik, Iran, that the idea occurred to Augustus Turnbull. Was it an idea or a realization . . . a goal toward which he had been moving unconsciously all his life?

Old Rinaldi was dead. His *other son,* Teodoro, *little Teodoro,* was alive. Over the years, Augustus had heard Teodoro was in school in Switzerland, in school in America, assigned to the legation in London. Skiing, yachting, playing polo. He was being groomed for the highest posts in His Majesty's government. *Precious little Teodoro.*

The idea was so grand, so basic, so simple that lying on his flea-infested bed, he felt it between his legs.

Infiltrate and destroy.

He would wipe out the Rinaldi family. Nice and slow. He would give himself the pleasure of doing it.

Nineteen months later, Augustus Turnbull changed employers again.

He used everything he had: having been born in that nation, having been trained by British Intelligence, having an intimate knowledge of the politics and the sewers of the Middle East, the Persian Gulf. He was accepted readily into His Majesty's Intelligence Service. Within three years of his decision in Sirik he was chief of His Majesty's secret intelligence wing in the United States.

And Teodoro Rinaldi, married, with a child, a son,

was stationed in the United States as Ambassador to the United Nations.

Faithful to the King—oh, Colonel Augustus Turnbull had been faithful to the King, was faithfully doing the legwork, the blackmail and the bribery, to get Resolution 1176R passed in the United Nations, when along came his old friend from mercenary days Simon Cord with a proposition, an idea so grand, so basic, so simple, again Augustus Turnbull felt it between his legs. . . .

Eleven

In the lobby of San Francisco's Fairmont Hotel, Spike put a quarter into a pay phone, carefully dialed O, the Manhattan exchange and then the number.

The operator said, "May I help you, please?"

"Yeah. Oh. This is a collect call."

"Your name, sir?"

"Ah—Wilkins."

"Thank you, sir. I'm ringing. Will you talk with anyone?"

Spike said, "Just the guy who answers."

A few meters away from him sat Tobias Rinaldi. His back was straight, his hands folded in his lap. Near him on the divan sat a girl in a brown velvet suit and leather boots reading *Vogue*.

Toby was looking at her.

"Jeez," Spike said into the phone. "That kid's used to bein' pushed around."

"Pardon me, sir?" the operator asked.

"I wasn't speakin' to you."

"There doesn't seem to be an answer, sir."

"There hasta be."

"Well, there isn't, sir. No one seems to be answering."

"What number did I give you—I mean, dial?"

The operator recited the number.

"Yeah, that's right."

"Would you like me to try it again?"

"Yeah. There must be some mistake. The guy said he'd be there. This number."

"Very good, sir."

Again, there was the ringing. The girl who had been sitting next to Toby was gone and Toby was looking down at his fingers as if he'd never seen them before.

"Jeez, what a punk kid."

"Sir? There is no answer at that number."

"Oh, yeah? How can that be?"

"I don't know, sir."

"Aw, okay, operator. But don't go home yet. I'll try later."

Twelve

Christina dragged her suitcases from her rented car in the parking lot down the long, dark path between a high hedge and the All Stars' Tennis Camp's staff bungalows. The young woman who showed Christina to the bungalow referred to the path as "Slave Alley." As a guest, Christina had never noticed the area or known of its existence. A party was going on in one of the other bungalows. Music was playing softly over the murmur of voices.

She stayed under a hot shower a long time, hoping it would relax her, make her feel better.

It didn't.

In her robe she sat on the lumpy divan, glancing frequently at her wristwatch, observing time stand still. Next to the divan was the telephone.

The bungalow was tiny. There was a Pullman kitchen, a bathroom with shower, a bedroom barely big enough for the bed and a dresser, and the living room with one long couch, two wicker chairs and a pine coffee table. There was no air conditioning.

On the walls were posters of the two popular model-filmstars of the moment, in poses more athletic than seductive, a T-shirt tacked up by its shoulders saying FOREST HILLS, an autographed tennis schedule and a large number of fly stains.

In every corner of the bungalow, it seemed, was something discarded—one sneaker, one sock, an empty rum bottle, a torn tennis magazine, a cracked Frisbee, a pair of blue jeans torn at the crotch.

Christina thought of getting up and finding something to eat. She felt slightly nauseous.

Again she glanced at her watch.

There was a rapping on the window of the bungalow door. Hearing it, the only immediate thought she had was that the pane of glass was loose in its frame.

Someone rapped again.

Remaining seated, Christina called out, "He's not here. Mark's away—at a tennis tournament."

Outside, a voice said, "Mrs. Rinaldi?"

"Yes." She got up. "Yes."

She opened the door.

A heavy man in a bulky tweed suit stood on the path.

"I'm Mrs. Rinaldi," she said.

"Augustus Turnbull, ma'am. Colonel Augustus Turnbull. Here to do anything I can to help."

"Oh, yes. Come in. Please."

After he entered, she saw that his tweed suit was green.

"I'm alone," she heard herself say.

"Your husband mentioned me?"

"Yes, I think he did. I don't know. He mentioned someone would be here. I'm so—"

"You're in a state of shock, Mrs. Rinaldi. A terrible state of shock. Over this terrible thing that has happened to your family."

"I was hoping someone would appear. I—I'm not thinking too well."

"Of course."

"I'm not sure what I'm supposed to be doing just now. I don't know what I can do."

She had difficulty seeing the man's eyes in his fat face.

"I don't think there's anything to be done just now. Get some sleep. We both need sleep."

"But Toby could be anywhere . . . anything could be happening to him."

Turnbull put his hand on her arm. "You can't think that way, Mrs. Rinaldi. I'm here now. Everything will be all right."

"That's very kind," she said. "But I don't know what it means."

"There are people in Washington and New York working on this, and there'll be more in the morning. Have you eaten? Would you like a drink? A sedative?"

"No. I don't want anything."

"This is very difficult." Turnbull moved around the living room, apparently seeing everything.

He picked up a broken tennis racket and went to one corner of the room. Stooping, he picked something up with the racket's handle. Christina saw it was a jock strap. Turnbull carried it to the door and threw it outside.

She smiled at him.

"There's one bed, I suppose?" he asked. "One bedroom?"

"Yes."

"I'll sleep there. On the couch." He could not conceal his look of dismay.

"There are no other rooms available," she said, "but there are motels nearby. I'll be all right."

"I'd rather stay with you," he said quietly, "for what comfort I may be to you."

"You really needn't."

"That's all right, Mrs. Rinaldi." He asked, "May I call you Christina?"

"Yes." She looked away. "Of course."

"All right, then. Good night, Christina. Try to sleep."

At the bedroom door, she said, "And what do we do? What do we do in the morning?"

"I'll need to make some phone calls," he answered. "I'll need to go out for a while. Don't you worry yourself. Just follow your own instincts. Leave everything in my hands."

Christina looked at his hands. The backs of his hands faced forward.

"All right. . . ." she said.

"Not to worry, Christina. We'll find your child. Believe me."

Thirteen

"Anyway—" Toby sat on the edge of the bed in Room 102 in the Red Star-Silvermine Motel continuing to tell the story he had begun in the car with Spike. Spike had never seemed much interested in it.

When they had arrived at the motel, Spike had left Toby in the car while he talked to the man in the office.

Spike and Toby had gone to the room alone.

Over the phone, Spike had ordered cheeseburgers, french fries and milk for them both.

Then he made another call. He dialed a lot of numbers, told the operator it was to be a collect call and said his name was Wilkins. He held the phone to his ear a long time before hanging up. There was no answer.

As Toby talked, Spike prowled around the room, looking in the closets, out the window, walking in and out of the bathroom several times.

Toby thought telling Spike a story might make him more peaceful. Stories always made Toby more peaceful.

"This policeman says to this newspaper reporter, Clark Kent, who really is Superman, you see, in different clothes—do you remember my telling you that, Spike?—'If we don't catch this crook soon, we can wave goodbye to all decency in this city!' I told you, Spike, that this terrible crook was stealing buses right off the city streets so everybody had to walk to the store. He would go disguised as a bus driver, you see, and knock out the real bus driver and then drive the bus away. He was selling them to some poor city in

China. They could never catch him because all bus
drivers look the same in their bus driver's uniforms—"

Spike turned from the window. "Shut up, kid. Go to
the bathroom."

"What?"

"Get into the bathroom."

"I went when I came in."

"Get into the bathroom!" Spike put his head too
close to Toby's, his glass eye staring. "Or I will twist
off two of your fingers and make you eat 'em!"

Toby wrinkled his nose. He put his hands in his
pockets.

He went into the bathroom.

*

"Lissen," Spike said. They were sitting on the edges
of their beds, eating the cheeseburgers and french
fries. Each had a pint of milk on the floor by his feet.
"Sick of your stories. Fac' is, you don't know what
you're talkin' about. How old are you? Twelve years
old?"

Pleased, Toby said, "No."

"How old?"

"Eight."

"Eight years old. Shit. I don't even remember eight
years ago hardly. Eight years is nothin'." He tried to
snap his fingers, but they were too greasy. "Eight
years means nothin'. What you ever done?"

"I done plenty," Toby said. He looked up from under his eyebrows at Spike. "I mean, I have done
plenty."

"Yeah? You don' sound it. You sound like an ignoramus kid."

"I've done plenty. I go to school."

"Everybody goes to school," Spike said. "Mos'ly."

"I've done the quad in under three. I'm age champion in the hundred-yard dash. . . ."

" 'Done the quad in under three.' What kinda language is that?"

"Yes. And I've studied French—"

"Who needs to speak French? Everybody I ever come across speak one of those crazy languages all you have to do is say shut up to, and if they don't, you punch 'em out. Stupid shits."

"I can sail a Beetle Cat—"

"Anybody can do that! You pick it up by its stupid tail, swing it through the air and let go! 'Sail a cat.' Fancy Dan talk."

"In Gstaad last year, skiing with His Majesty, they allowed me on the medium-advanced slopes. That's pretty good for a kid my age. And it wasn't because of anything His Majesty said, either."

"What's a Gstaad? Ko-zum-tite!"

"It's a place we go skiing. With His Majesty."

"Who's 'His Majesty'? Your old man?"

"Old man?"

"Your father?"

"No. The King."

" 'The King.' Jeez, ignoramus kid."

"Sure. And the King has put me on some of his ponies. He even had a special short mallet made for me."

"What for? What's a mallet?"

"For polo."

"Jeez, kid. Ignoramus kid. Fancy Dan talk. You're outa your tree. Fac' is, you've had too much of that red horse."

"What red horse?"

"That red-horse stuff you were always talkin' about on the plane. In your suitcase."

"That's Red Pony."

"There's a diff'runce?"

"Where is my suitcase?"

"I tol' ya, kid. Fac' is, the airlines lost it. You need a fix, kid? Ahh, you don't know what you're talkin' about. Fac' is, you confuse me."

"I don't have any clothes. Any pajamas. Any clothes for the morning."

"What'sa matter with the clothes you got on?"

Toby looked down at the sleeves of his jacket. "I've been wearing them all day."

" 'Wearing 'em all day'! I wear clothes two, three weeks. Then I throw them away."

"Two, three weeks at a time?"

"Yeah. See, I got money now. I can do that."

"Don't you itch?"

"When I itch, I go to the store."

"So that's why you don't have any luggage, either?"

"That's right, kid. Travel light. On the road. Keep movin'."

"Why wasn't my mother at that big hotel we went to?"

"You already ast me that."

"In the car I said, 'Where's my mother?' and you didn't answer."

"You saw me on the phone?"

"Of course I saw you on the phone."

"Fac' is, they tol' me she couldn't make it. She was gonna be late. Real late. Maybe two, three days late."

"Oh. You were talking with my mother?"

"No. 'Course not. The airlines. I was talkin' to the people at the airlines. 'Cause your mother wasn't at the hotel, see?"

Toby said, "You never asked at the desk."

"Fac' is, she supposed to be waitin' for us in the lobby, see? So I called the airlines."

"Oh."

"They said to come over here. Cheaper, you know? Who needs a big hotel like that?"

"But if my mother's going there—"

"Oh, yeah, kid. When she arrives, she'll call us here. That's why we're supposed to stay here, see? Wait for her to call us. Then we'll go back to that other hotel." Spike ran his index finger around his teeth, wiped his fingers on his pants and smiled at Toby. "See? You don't know everything. Just an ignoramus kid."

Toby said, "I need a toothbrush."

"In the morning, kid. Maybe we'll get things in the morning."

"Pajamas?"

"Shit, no. Pajamas is for sissies."

Toby said, "Why?"

"Why? I dunno. 'Cause you don' know much, that's why. Just an ignoramus kid. Swingin' a cat—"

"Sailing a cat."

"We used to call it swingin' a cat. You don't think I never swung a cat?" His eyes narrowed. "Lissen, you pour kerosene on it, set a match to it, set the cat on fire, then you swing it by its tail over your head a few times. Then you let go."

Toby felt his blood fall down through his body.

"You never did that, did you, kid?"

Toby swallowed hard.

"See? Fac' is, you don' know nothin'. Nothin' at all. This stuff you make up. His Majesty. The King. Jeez, kid."

"There is a King."

"There are no kings."

"My father works for him."

"Yeah? You're full of bullshit."

"There are lots of kings."

"There are no kings. They're called presidents nowadays, stupid. Fac' is, I even been in some places they call 'em *presidentes*. There are no kings, but I can tell you some real stories. You want to hear some real stories?"

They were surrounded by greasy cheeseburger wrappings, french fries containers, milk cartons. Toby was looking from one scrap to another. He was thinking about going to bed without pajamas.

Uncertainly, he said, "Sure."

"Okay." Hands behind his head, Spike lay back on his bed. "Fac' is, there are no crooks, either."

Toby said, "Oh."

"Just guys who have a job to do, makin' a livin' at what they can, like bankrobbin' or knockin' over a liquor store, burglarin', like that. It's a profession, see? Like, I'll bet your daddy is a banker or somethin', isn't he? Rich guy?"

Toby hesitated. "He talks to people."

"See? Okay. He's a salesman. That's his profession. Other people rob. Run numbers. Sharks. That's their business. See? It all works out. Everybody has kids, see."

"You have kids?"

"I dunno. None nobody ever tol' me about." Spike laughed. "And there's no Superman, neither. There are cops, sure, but they don't go flyin' through the air in no big cape." Looking at Toby, Spike's good eye glinted. "Mos'ly, they sit in the middle doin' as well as they can for themselves, if you get what I mean, takin' anythin' that comes down the pike." He continued to look at Toby. "I see you don' unnerstand me. Lemme say this: people you call cops are always botherin' people tryin' to make their way. Got that?"

Toby ran his eyes over the scraps of paper and cardboard again.

Spike returned to examining the ceiling. "Fac' is, there was this cop in Newark—this big, fat cop, a detective, belly hangin' over his belt, life had been so good to him, big, fat belly. And he shot a frien' of mine. Kilt him. That wasn't fair. All this frien' of mine was doin' was takin' things outa a warehouse after dark. Nothin' to get kilt about. The cop said my frien' had a gun and pulled it. See, that isn't fair, Toby. The cop shoulda least let my frien' get off a shot or two at him before he shot him dead. Right?

"So what they do in a case like this—when a cop shoots somebody they give him a vacation, a kinda reward, only they call it a suspension and they have a big investigation while everybody forgets about it ever happening, and so they can say, sure, it was all right for the cop to shoot ol' Joe or Pete or whatever the stiff's name. You probably know all this from television. You gotta know something. Where you been all your life? Eight years old!"

Sitting on the edge of a bed in a San Francisco motel, Toby's eyes began to close. He was hot. Only two days before he had been in school in New Hampshire.

"But I didn't forget. This particular guy was a frien' o' mine.

"So while this particular big, fat cop was on vacation, I hung aroun' outside his house one morning. He came out. Swimming suit. Beach towels. Six-pack beer. Put the stuff in the trunk of his car. Nice vacation. Shot somebody so he got to go to the beach.

"I follow him down outside Red Bank. Watch him take a swim, swallow couple beers, begin to settle down on the beach.

"Hour or so later, he stands up, all hot and sweaty, jumps in the ocean again, starts back.

"Only, I'm on the beach with my knife. Big knife."

Through his eyelashes Toby watched Spike show with his hands how big a knife it was.

"He looks at me funny like, 'cause I'm the only one on the beach in clothes."

"Anyway, I stick the knife into the top of his big belly, push it sideways and down. Then I do the same with the other side of his stomach. Make a big flap, you know? Then I stuck my fingers in along the top of the flap, grabbed a lota flesh and guts and pulled down.

"With him lookin' down at himself, all his guts spillin' out on the beach."

For an instant, Toby saw Spike clearly, very clearly—more clearly than he had ever seen anything or anyone before. Then he saw Spike lurch, the room heave.

Spike said, "I didn't stay for a swim. It was a hot day, too."

Toby ran for the bathroom.

Kneeling by the toilet, vomiting cheeseburger, french fries, milk, he heard Spike in the bedroom laughing so hard he was coughing for breath.

*

"Hey, kid. You awake?"

In his bed in the dark motel room, Toby was awake. He was naked. He was hungry.

He didn't answer.

Spike said, "I tol' ya I'd tell ya a story. A *real* story."

Fourteen

"I don't know," Ria Marti said.

In the back of the limousine she was sitting on the right-hand side. The car was oozing up the Avenue of the Americas. It was quarter to eleven at night.

The Ambassador had gotten himself through a long cocktail party at the Italian Embassy. He had even had a forty-five minute private consultation with the Japanese Ambassador in the Embassy's library. They had gone on to the CBS television studio, where the Ambassador had taped an interview for the next day's morning news.

Neither had had anything much to eat. Ria thought Teddy unusually pale.

"You don't know what?" Rinaldi asked absently.

"I'm sitting on some kind of a powder keg," Ria said. "And I don't know what it is."

"What makes you think so?"

"You can't be public relations officer for an embassy without developing a sixth sense. Something's wrong, and I know it."

"First time I've ever heard you plead female intuition."

"It's more than that. I suspect you almost goofed."

"Oh? How?"

"When Roger Mudd asked you if His Majesty has a secret police force to keep track of students and radicals. . . ."

"I get asked that all the time. Funny how some rumors never die."

"And you deny it all the time."

"I denied it tonight."

Ria put her hand on his. "Teddy, you hesitated. You licked your lips. When you answered, your mouth was dry."

He took his hand away and said nothing.

"You can't get away with that on television," she said. "Just wait. Tomorrow every news group in the country will call with the same damned question."

They were being driven by Louis, the Jamaican.

"Something is going on," he said.

She said, "Is it Toby?"

He said, "Wait until we get to the Residence."

*

The houseman-valet, Pav, as usual, was on late-night duty. He had set out cold sandwiches and brandy in the library.

After the library door was closed, Ria handed Teddy a plate of sandwiches and a brandy and soda.

The hand that took the sandwich plate was shaking. He put the plate down, drank half the brandy and soda, went to the side table and refilled the glass.

Ria watched him silently.

"Guess I'm not very good at my job," he said.

"In fact," she said, sitting on the divan and drawing her legs up, "you are."

"Funny," he said. "The boss wasn't too pleased by my marrying an American citizen. Especially an American girl with the Christian name Christina."

Ria was just listening.

"Yet he expressed enough joy when Toby was born. Regarded him almost as one of his own sons."

"Toby," Ria said.

Teddy drew a deep breath. "Toby is missing."

Ria sat up, putting her feet on the floor.

"We're pretty sure kidnapped. Mrs. Brown put him on the plane to San Francisco this afternoon. He did not get off the plane. Christina was waiting to meet him."

"Oh, Teddy! God! How *awful*!"

Teddy shrugged at the inadequacy of the word.

"The Resolution," Ria said.

"I've had a call. Ria, Toby's dead if I submit the Resolution."

"Teddy, Teddy," Ria said.

"So . . ."

"Is Christina returning?"

Teddy hesitated. "Not at the moment. Makes more sense to leave her out there—where Toby knows she is." He turned his back on Ria. "The point is . . ." He choked. " . . . we don't know where Toby is."

"Oh, Teddy."

She started across the room toward him, but he turned abruptly.

"Regarding the press, Ria: no notice of this is to be given out. The Residence staff, of course, knows about it because most of them had been questioned. They've been sworn to silence. For Toby's sake, your staff and the Embassy staff in general is not to know about it. There are to be no leaks."

"I'll take care of it," she said.

"Business as usual. To get the Resolution accepted, it is imperative no one thinks this Embassy is under any particular strain. If the press should make any inquiries on this matter, you are to stonewall them absolutely. Toby is at Fantazyland with his mother."

"Don't worry about that part of it," Ria said. "I'll do my job."

"I know. I'm sure of it."

"What's being done?" she asked. "You haven't gone to the local police, have you? You couldn't have. The F.B.I.?"

"No." He looked into his brandy glass. "No."

"Oh!" she said. Her eyes grew wide. "Oh! It is true!"

Teddy was looking at her blankly.

"That's why you clutched up on television!"

"I deny it." Teddy put down his glass. "His Majesty's government does not have a secret intelligence arm in this country."

"And you never knew it!" She collapsed on the divan. "I never knew it. It's true!"

Teddy said, "Some jobs are more difficult than others."

"Are they any good?" she asked. "I mean, is this the best way . . . ?"

Teddy said, "They haven't made a good impression on me so far, but I don't know. Don't seem to have many choices just now."

He gave himself more brandy, this time adding soda.

"Look, Ria. I'd rather be left alone just now. I suspect we've got long days ahead of us. . . ."

She stood up immediately.

"Can't I help you, Teddy? Are you sure you wouldn't want me to stay with you tonight?"

"Thanks," he said. "No."

"It might be a good idea," she said.

"Yes," he said. "It might be."

"Then let me stay."

"No," he said. "Somehow it would be too . . . I don't know, Ria . . . significant?"

Fifteen

The beam from Cord's penlight ran down the chipped directory in the outer lobby of the apartment house on New York's West Eighty-ninth Street. It stopped at "4C—Du—owski."

Cord did not ring the bell. He pressed the palm of his gloved hand against the glass door. It swung open.

In the dimly lit lobby, he found the door to the fire stairs next to the elevator. It being quarter past three in the morning, he used the stairs. He did not know what he would find, or do, in Apartment 4C, but he did not want restless residents of the building remembering they heard someone using the elevator at that hour.

The fourth-floor corridor walls were yellow veneered brick. There was the smell of fish.

The door to 4C was locked. Again, he did not ring the bell. He kicked the door handle hard with his heel. The door sprang open, bounced off the wall.

There were no lights on in the apartment.

Cord entered and closed the door.

"Dubrowski?" he said quietly.

With his penlight he found a light switch and clicked it on.

There was one camp chair next to a floor lamp facing a small, portable television set on its own packing crate. There was a record player, five or six albums propped against it. Against one wall was a large, cheap mirror. Strewn on the floor in front of it on a six-by-six plastic mat was a complete set of weights. The place smelled of stale sweat.

Cord switched on the bedroom light before entering. Against the far wall near the windows were stacks

of magazines. There were also two or three cardboard
containers of Kaufmann's Hi-Protein tablets. Next to
the head of the bed a telephone was on an orange
crate. On the floor right next to the cot was a pair of
hand weights.

There were also a hypodermic syringe, a tablespoon
with a blackened bowl, a paper packet of matches, a
half dozen burned-out matches on the floor, and four
clear plastic packets. Only one of the packets was
empty.

Dubrowski was on the cot. His eyes were open, the
pupils angled oddly, downward, toward the floor. His
teeth were deep in his tongue. The tip of his tongue
was purple. There was dried blood on his teeth.

He was naked. Dubrowski was broad shouldered,
thin hipped. There was not an ounce of fat on him.
His pectoral, stomach, thigh and calf muscles had
been highly developed.

He was in tip-top shape, for a corpse—for someone
who had OD'd.

Cord turned off the lights and left the apartment,
closing the door behind him.

Sixteen

Christina was awake. She had spent the night awake, staring at the bedroom ceiling, trying not to think of what might be happening to Toby, not to sob out loud. If Colonel Turnbull hadn't been on the living room couch, she would have turned on her light, gotten up, taken another warm shower, prowled around. Instead she had passed the night listening to him through the thin door, snoring, coughing.

Shortly after dawn she heard him get up, rumble around the living room. The only access to the bathroom was through her bedroom.

The bungalow's front door closed, and then there was silence.

Christina got up and went into the living room. The sofa looked more lumpy than ever. It looked like it had been through a wrestling match with a bear.

It was too early to call Teddy in New York. She was sure he wasn't sleeping, either. But she was also sure he would call her if there had been any news.

"Just follow your own instincts," Colonel Turnbull had said.

Christina returned to the bedroom to get dressed.

Seventeen

At five minutes past seven in the morning, Toby walked into the lobby of the Red Star-Silvermine Motel.

There was a man behind the reception desk, seventy years old or more, sorting slips of paper. His head was bald on top but white hair fluffed out over his ears.

Toby said to him, "Where's the silver mine?"

The man said, "You're lookin' at it. I'm the Silvermine. My name could be Goldmine or Platinummine, I suppose, but the natural humility of my family limited their aspirations. Still, better to be a Silvermine than a Coppermine or a Coalmine, I've always figured. I'm one of the natural wonders of California, son. Right up there with Disneyland, Fantazyland and Hollywood. I'm a walkin' Silvermine."

"I'm going to Fantazyland," Toby said.

"Are you, now? Better watch out those mechanical crocodiles don't get a bite of you." Silvermine put down his sorted papers. "Nothin's worse than bein' bitten by a crocodile with automatic dentures."

"Have you even been bitten by a mechanical crocodile?"

"'Course! How do you suppose my hair got this way? When I was bit, the ouch was so bad my hair shot out over my ears and it's been stuck out that way ever since. You wouldn't want your hair to look like this, would you?"

"No, sir."

"I thought not. I haven't seen you before. You must be young Jackson. When your Pa came in last night, he just wrote in the register, 'Jackson, son.' I obliged

him to write down his first name and he wrote, 'Jack
Jackson, son.' I asked him to impart your name. He
wrote, 'Jack Jackson, son, Jack Jackson.' Are you Jack
Jackson, son, Jack Jackson's son?"

Toby didn't understand. He said, "My mother's
coming to get me. She's late. Then we're going to Fantazyland."

"Well, then, Jack Jackson, Jack Jackson's son. What
can I do for you? You're up early."

"The waitress said I had to ask you if I can charge
breakfast in the coffee shop."

"Old man not up yet, uh? Sure you can. Kids get
hungry whether other people are awake or asleep. I
remember that. Let's see, you're in Room 102, right?"

Mr. Silvermine came from behind the counter. He
was wearing plaid shorts and sandals.

"I'll come down and introduce you properly to the
waitress. How come you're dressed that way? Long
pants, blazer. Don't see many people 'round here
dressed that way. Least not kids. You'll be hot."

Going down the corridor, Mr. Silvermine pointed
through a window. "You seen our swimming pool?"

"Yes," Toby said. "It's nice."

"That's a special kind of water we have in the swimming pool, you know. You jump into it and you're
guaranteed to get wet. All over. Try it. You might like
it."

"Where can we buy things?"

"Like what?"

"Toothbrush. Pajamas. Clothes."

"You guys travel light, uh? Sure you're not a couple
of desperadoes? Bank robbers on the lam?"

"My luggage got lost. On the airplane."

"Oh. Well, that's how they keep airplanes flyin', you
know. They feed 'em a whole mess of luggage, and
the airplane chews it all up and just spits out what it
don't want. Luggage is airplane condiments. Gives

'em energy. I guess your particular airplane found your suitcase mighty tasty. Anyway, there's a shopping center across the road." As he walked, Mr. Silvermine waved his hand over his shoulder. "Get anything you want there. Only, you'd better drive across. Motorists don't respect you enough to slow down for you unless you're wrapped in just as much tin as they are."

"If a telephone call comes for us and we're at the pool, would you let us know?"

"Better'n that. I'd transfer the call out to you."

"My mother's going to call," Toby said.

Mr. Silvermine said to the waitress: "This is Jack Jackson, Jack Jackson's son. Feed him up and put it on the bill for Room 102. This young man's goin' to Fantazyland, and we ought to fatten him up for the crocodiles. An airplane's already eaten his luggage."

*

Toby had to knock several times on the door to Room 102.

Finally, hair tousled, a towel wrapped around him, Spike opened the door.

Both his eyes were wide, staring. His mouth was slightly open.

He looked up and down the corridor quickly, grabbed Toby by the neck and yanked him into the room.

"How did you get out? Where did you go?"

"I went to breakfast."

"Jeez!"

"I was hungry."

"You're supposed to stay with me!"

"You were asleep."

"I know I was asleep. I'm supposed to sit up with you all night, starin' at cha? Fac' is, you're a dumb kid!"

Quietly, Toby said, "I got breakfast."

"Stay there! Don't move a Goddamned inch!"

"I lost my supper last night!"

Before going into the shower, Spike said, "You stay there!"

Toby stayed there.

*

When Spike came out of the shower, Toby said, "Spike? When you take a shower, do you take the glass eye out of your head first?"

"Jeez!"

"I just want to know."

Spike said, "It's not gonna be hard to twist your head off. Fac' is, it'll be a pleasure."

He began getting dressed.

"There's a swimming pool," Toby said.

Spike said nothing.

"Special kind of water. Guaranteed to get you wet."

Spike looked at him.

"It's a nice day," Toby said. "Sun's out. Hot."

Spike checked his hair in the mirror.

"There's a place across the street. A shopping center. We can get all kinds of things there. Pajamas. Toothbrushes. Clothes. Swim suits."

"You think you know everythin', doncha?"

"I went on an explore." Toby giggled. "I even found the Silvermine."

"Well, you don' know nothin'. Fac' is, I'm goin' for breakfast. And you're goin' to stay here. Then we're goin' to stay in this room until we get a telephone call. Until your mother calls." Spike checked his pants pocket for the room key. He switched on the television. "Here, you look at T.V. See if you can learn somethin'."

After Spike left, Toby heard the sound of the key in

the lock. On the television a man in a yellow suit was telling the story of Moses in the bulrushes. "*And Pharaoh charged all his people, saying, Every son that is born ye shall cast into the river, and every daughter ye shall save alive. . . .*"

Toby got off the bed and went to the door. He tried the handle. The door opened. No one was in the corridor. He went back into the room, pushed a chair into line with the television and sat down.

"*And Pharaoh's daughter said to her, Go. And the maid went and called the child's mother. . . .*"

Eighteen

"Mr. Ambassador?"

Sylvia Menninges's voice blurted through the intercom. Again, Teddy had been sitting at his desk, staring at his wastebasket.

"Yes."

"Assistant Secretary of State Skinner. Line 253."

"Yes." He picked up the phone. "Yes?"

"Teddy! How goes the battle?"

Teddy remembered he was to be hearty with Pat Skinner. Characteristically hearty. He and Pat had known each other since Government 101 at Harvard. They were friends. Which was why Patrick Skinner had been named Assistant Secretary of State when Teodoro Rinaldi had been named Ambassador to the United Nations: almost exclusively to deal with Teddy.

The Ambassador tried to lighten his voice. "How be Frannie and the little skinnies?"

It was stupid of him to ask about Pat's wife and children. They had talked just after lunch yesterday.

"Teddy, what's the matter?"

"Guess I didn't sleep too well last night."

"Well, you must be relieved at the good news this morning."

"What good news?"

"Monday night. You get to introduce your Resolution Monday night."

"Oh."

"You didn't know that?"

"No."

"I should think your office would have had that information by seven thirty this morning. Don't they check?"

Teddy's eyes wandered slowly to his desk calendar. *It's Friday noon.*

"I mean, it's sort of imperative you know how much more time you have to negotiate."

Indeed, Teddy thought, *to negotiate the life of my son.*

"How did the meeting with the Iranian bunch go this morning?"

"I'm sorry?"

"The Iranian delegation. You said you were going to meet with them at eight thirty."

". . . I didn't see them."

"Oh. You were meeting with the East German delegation at ten."

Teddy said, "I didn't."

The extension buttons on his telephone had been flashing all morning, but Teddy had been only dimly aware of them. *They've been leaving me alone! The staff has been leaving me alone. Damn, dear Ria Marti. Now they all must know something's wrong.*

"Mr. Ambassador," Pat Skinner said. "You have a bit of a hangover this morning, or something?"

"Yes," Teddy said. "It's possible. Something like that."

"Well, you have the weekend," Pat said.

"Yes. I have the weekend," Teddy said. "Pat, I'll call you back."

*

Pat Skinner walked into the enormous office of the Secretary of State. The Secretary, coat off, shoes off, was sitting back in a recliner lounge near the fireplace, reading. His briefcase was open on the floor beside him.

"Morning," Pat said. "Just talked with Rinaldi."

"And how's Rinaldi?"

"Showing signs of stress."

"Oh?"

"His concert's Monday night. Eight P.M."

"Resolution 1176R. . . . " the Secretary said, "to work longer, harder, more intelligently . . . diplomatically—if I may use such a stupid word—than Teddy Rinaldi has on Resolution 1176R."

"All that won't do any good, Mr. Secretary, if when the curtain goes up, ol' Teddy can't play his fiddle."

"That bad?"

"Stress level seven . . . nine. . . ."

"This whole world," the Secretary said, "is run, always, by tired people. People who eat a little too much, drink a little too much, take a few too many pills, sleep too little. History," he said, looking over the rims of his glasses, "is nothing more than the best arrangements that can be achieved by tired minds."

"Just thought I'd alert you," Pat said.

"It would be too bad if we had to back away from this Resolution, from supporting it."

"It would."

"Which of course we'll have to do if you tell me Teddy's chances of carrying it off are slipping."

Pat Skinner took a deep breath. "I know."

The Secretary of State said, "Keep me informed."

&

Alone in his office, Teddy was staring off into space. Earlier that morning, Mrs. Brown had come into the dining room where he was breakfasting alone.

"Nobody slept," she said. "I spent the night awake. Whatever I did, it wasn't sleepin'. No more the same for you, Mr. Ambassador."

Her presence made him put some egg in his mouth.

"Oh, I had some horrible thoughts. I'm sure we all did." She was pretending to do something at the sideboard—straighten something. "But I had some good thoughts, too, Mr. Ambassador. You know your son is a rare cookie."

The egg yoke wouldn't stay on his fork.

"Is he?"

"Indeed he is, sir. He can handle himself, take care of himself, better than anyone would suspect. A genius at handling people. Put him in almost any situation, sir, and he never loses sight of his direction. Remember his wantin' to go to that sailin' camp? And the time he wanted that Egyptian boy to stay with him when our two countries weren't precisely talkin' that week? Well, sir, I tell you. If there's a way out, don't be too surprised if Toby finds it for himself."

The Ambassador knew Mrs. Brown had been awake all night trying to think of something to say to make himself, Christina, the staff feel better.

He also knew his son, Toby, was only eight years old.

Standing by the kitchen door, innocent blue eyes sad, she said, "Now, what should I do about the carpets, sir?"

"Carpets?"

"Yes, sir."

He stood up from the dining room table.

"I don't care. Give 'em to the Salvation Army."

Nineteen

In Room 102 at the Red Star-Silvermine Motel, Spike and Toby were on their beds.

On the television there was a game show.

The telephone had not rung.

The air conditioner was making a boring noise.

At breakfast, Spike had bought a newspaper he had been reading ever since. The headline read: WOMAN KEEPS HER BABY'S SKULL IN PURSE SEVENTEEN YEARS. The one under that read: STARS PREDICT FALL FROM HORSE FOR EX-PRESIDENT'S WIFE—*Your. Horoscope, page 36.* I'LL NEVER LOVE AGAIN, *Says Teenaged Star of TV's "There's Always Tomorrow."* Spike was taking a half hour to read each page.

"Spike?"

No answer.

"I'm hot."

On the TV, people were guessing whether a particular young husband had ever tried on his wife's brassiere.

"What's a brassiere?"

"Dumb kid. Don't know nothin' 'bout nothin'."

It turned out the young man *had* tried on his wife's brassiere, and everyone laughed including the young man. Someone referred to it just as a bra. Toby knew what a bra was.

He got up and opened the drapes. A wide shaft of sunlight came into the room. It bleached the images on the TV screen. The noon news was coming on. Toby turned the TV off and flopped on his bed, belly down.

"Swim," Toby said. "Pool."

Spike said nothing.

"Place across the street. We can get toothpaste, swimming trunks, pajamas. Only, Mr. Silvermine says we have to drive across, because of the traffic."

"Who's Mr. Silvermine?"

"The owner. He wears shorts."

Spike's look was sharp. "You talked with him?"

"Had to. To get breakfast."

Spike shook his head. "Jeez."

Aloud, Toby read a headline from an inside page of the newspaper: "*War Predicted for Persian Gulf. President Terms Oil Flow Essential for Free World Survival.* What does that mean, Spike?"

"Means you're a dumb kid what don' know nothin' 'bout nothin'," Spike muttered.

"Oh," Toby said. "I see." Smiling, he put his face against his arms. "I get it now," he said. "Anyway, I know what a bra is."

Spike had unbuttoned his shirt.

"Spike? You like stayin' in a room, just one little room like this, all the time?"

"Fac' is, I'm used to it."

Toby said, "So am I."

"Sure, kid. You been in jail, too. Right?"

Toby lifted his head. "You been in jail?"

Spike shrugged. "Like everybody else. Twic't."

"For tearing that man's stomach off?"

"Naw. They never caught me for that. The guy croaked. They never caught me for a lot of things. Just chicken-shit stuff."

"Like what? What'd they catch you for?"

"Oh, when I was fourteen I borried a car. Somethin' was wrong with the steerin', you know? So I went a block or two and smashed into another car. Knocked me silly. So when the cops arrived, there I was, high as a grasshopper, asleep at the wheel. Unconscious. Reformed school for me." Spike had put the newspaper aside. "For two years I had to eat burned rice. A lot a wet, burned rice."

"We get rice at school."

"Not wet, burned rice."

"Wet, burned rice."

"Not a lot of it."

"A lot of it."

"Other time, I was just outa reformed school. I was hungry. You never been hungry."

"I been hungry."

"No money. Unemployed. Who'd hire a kid who'd been in jail? All day I'd been waiting, you know? Money, food come from somewhere. Well, it didn't. Ten thirty at night, I couldn't stand it no more. Waited outside a bar. Decided to mug the next guy who came out. Well, fac' is, I did, and fac' is, he was a cop. Bye, bye, Spike, so long, nice to know ya. That place even had rice soup. You know, water with rice in it?"

"I know."

"Whadda you know?"

"What's jail like?"

"Spend a lot of time locked in a room. Even have the crapper in there so you smell yourself all the time; don't have no place to go. No toilet seat. 'Fraid you'd wear it as a necklace or somethin'. Sit around the machine shop. Sit around the cell. Shavin' and takin' a shower, fresh clothes—things you really get to look forward to. And the guys you have to talk to! Stupid shits. If they weren't stupid, they wouldna got caught."

"You got caught."

Spike looked at him. "I was just a dumb kid. Like you. Didn't know nothin'. I know a lot more now than I did then. You'd better believe it. You don't see me in jail now, do you?"

"It seems like we're in jail."

"Well, we're not. I can walk outa this room anytime I want to."

"Why don't we?"

"You don't know what you're talkin' about. School. Home to Mommy. Cookie-milk anytime you want it. Hugs and kisses, sleep tight, don't let no skeeters bite."

"No."

"Whaddaya mean, 'no'?"

"I don't go to that kind of school. I don't live at home."

"If you don't live at home, where do you live?"

"School. I live at school."

"You live there?"

"Yeah."

"Alla time?"

"Mostly."

"No foolin'. What's it like?"

"Big. Heavy, gray stone."

"You have a room there?"

"A little room."

"But you're never locked in it."

"Sort of. Every afternoon from four thirty to six, I have to be in there doin' homework, and then again at night from seven thirty to nine. The lights go out at nine twenty, ready or not."

"Yeah."

"But where's the crapper?"

"Down the hall."

"You can go there anytime you want. . . ."

"You're not supposed to. If you're out of your room during those times and they catch you, you have to spend Sunday afternoon in detention hall."

"But you can take a crap?"

"You're supposed to before or after."

"Jeez! Strict! Can't even take a crap in your place or

it's solitary for you—no shit! What'd you ever do to get sent to a place like that?"

Toby shrugged. "I don't know. I'm gettin' a fine education, I guess."

"Sounds worse'n my reformed school. They feed you good?"

"Lot a rice," Toby said. "Lot a rice."

"Where is this place of yours?"

"New Hampshire."

"In the sticks?"

"What?"

"I mean, is it in the city or the woods?"

"Woods. Country."

"You mean, even when you look through the window there's nothin' to see? No girls? Just fuckin' trees?"

"I don't think the trees around there fuck." Toby smiled. "At least, I've never seen them."

"You know what fuck means?"

"Yeah," Toby said.

"Jeez. No wonder you're in reformed school, age of ten."

"Eight. I'm eight."

"Worse. And you never get to go anywhere? You never get to go home?"

"Sometimes. Ten days. Last summer I went to a sailing camp."

"Yeah, they were startin' the furlough program second place I was at. Just like your place. Out in the sticks."

"You know this motel has a swimming pool?" Toby said.

"I seen it."

"Mr. Silvermine says it has a special kind of water. I mean, in the swimming pool."

"Yeah?"

"Guaranteed to get you wet. All over."

"I don't swim so good."

"I can teach you. A little."

"I don't need you teachin' me nothin'."

"Hot in here, isn't it?"

Spike sighed. "Yeah. What's on the television?"

"Golf," said Toby.

"Anybody who watches golf on television is a birdie," said Spike.

"We can use the pool, you know," Toby said. "Because we're guests here."

"Yeah? I suppose so."

"Spike?"

"What."

"Let's go for a swim."

"Naw. Have to wait for the telephone."

"No, we don't. I asked Mr. Silvermine. He said if a call came for us, I mean, if my mother calls, he'd transfer the call out to the pool."

"You said what?"

"There's a telephone by the pool."

"Jeez, you had quite a chin wag with that old coot, didn't ya?"

"He's a nice man. Though I didn't understand a lot of what he said. He's been to Fantazyland, too."

"You tol' him you're goin' to Fantazyland?"

"Sure."

"What else did ya tell him?"

"Nothin'. Waitin' for my mother to call."

"Tha's good. Jeez, kid, you're dumb."

"Anyway," Toby said, "we could get swimming trunks and toothpaste and clothes at this place across the freeway."

"Jeez. Why didn't cha call the cops?"

"Cops? Why would I call the cops?"

"I dunno, kid. I dunno."

"Fact is, Spike, I need clothes. I'm hot. Mr. Silvermine says everybody here wears shorts. He wears shorts. He said you don't see many people around here dressed like this."

Spike tossed him a quick look. "He said that?"

"Yeah."

Spike was biting the end of his thumb. "You may be right, kid. At that. Yeah."

Spike sat up on the edge of his bed. "Yeah. Let's go get you some clothes. Fac' is, you don't look right. Not at all. And that's a fac'."

Toby jumped off the bed.

"And swimming trunks, and pajamas?"

"Yeah, yeah. Maybe."

"And then we'll go to the pool?"

"Yeah. Maybe. Dirty bastids. Allus puttin' us in a room and tellin' us to stay there. Fuck 'em's what I say."

"Right!" Toby said. "Fuck 'em!"

Twenty

"Dubrowski's OD'd," Cord said over the phone to Turnbull. "Like fish on ice."

"You gave money to a junkie before he did his job!"

"Okay, Gus. I made a mistake. We gotta work our way out of it."

"What do you mean, 'we'?"

"You want what you want, Gus, and I want what my employers want."

"So who snatched the kid?"

"Maybe a guy named Mullins. Spike Mullins. He and Dubrowski knew each other at Attica. Last night I went to this bar where I used to meet Dubrowski. I bought a lot of drinks, you know? Tuesday, Dubrowski was flying pretty high. Zonked. Wednesday, he was seen looking pretty seedy in a corner of the bar, talking to this jail buddy of his. The bartender said he saw Dubrowski hand Mullins a wad of bills. My guess is Dubrowski hired this buddy to stand in for him on the grab until he got himself together and got out to the Coast to take over."

"Then Dubrowski went home and OD'd."

"Yeah."

"So we don't know how to get in touch with Mullins and Mullins doesn't know how to get in touch with us."

"Yeah."

"You do nice work, Cord. What do you know about this Mullins?"

"Dumb and vicious. I got the people in the bar to tell me stories about him. A real psychotic thug."

"Another druggie?"

"No. Apparently not. Gus, we've got to find that kid."

"I will."

"I mean, what would you do if you were this guy Mullins and someone got you into a situation like this and then didn't follow through? I mean, you've got a kidnapped kid on your hands you don't know what to do with?"

"Kill him and dump him."

"Yeah. The kid is no good to us dead, Gus. At least until Monday night. I said you could do whatever you wanted to the kid—to the family—after Monday night. I mean, to Christina Rinaldi and the Ambassador and all. A dead kid's a dead threat."

"I don't see we have a deal anymore, Cord."

"Maybe I ought to come out to the Coast, Gus."

"Stay out of my way, Cord."

"We'll meet. We'll talk."

"Cord. Stay out of my way."

Twenty-one

"MARCO!"

"POLO!"

". . . MARCO!"

". . . POLO!"

Spike watched the kids play in the motel pool. They were all about the same size. Three boys and two girls. Wet, skinny, darting kids, faces, shoulders, arms, legs, flashing in the sunlight, their hair changing color and texture every time their heads came up from the water.

Sitting in a swim suit in a long chair, his legs stretched out before him, Spike finished his second beer.

"MARCO!"

". . . POLO!"

Across the pool under an umbrella sat a woman in a swim suit, knitting. Her yarn was in a plastic Sachs bag at her feet. At least one of the kids, one of the boys, belonged to her. He'd climb out to her once in a while, use a towel, stand in the shade of the umbrella, catch his breath. Occasionally, she would look up from her knitting at the kids in the pool and smile.

I ought to go give her a pound of the best. One-two-three behind your tree. Spike glowered at her and the rest of the world. *Bastids. Put me in a room, tell me to stay there. Cheap bastids.*

"MARCO!"

Spike figured the game the kids were playing had something to do with people who couldn't see so well. They'd grope around the pool for each other, in turn, as if blind. All the kids who had their eyes open would tease and taunt the person with his eyes closed—call to him loudly from close up, then swim away quickly and quietly.

Little bastids. Think it's funny bein' short of sight. Think it's funny never knowin' what's goin' on outa the left side of your head. . . .

"POLO!"

Spike's head lowered to the cushion. *Nice. Nice bein' out. Nice havin' a job to do, and doin' it. Nice bein' in the sun. Nice havin' a beer just 'cause you want it. . . .*

But where the hell is Dubrowski?

❁

"Come on," the boy said. "Want a Coke? Who wants a Coke?"

Standing in the pool, Toby looked at Spike asleep in the chair.

"No," he said. "I don't think so."

"Haven't you got any money?" The boy looked at Spike. "Oh, your dad's asleep. That's okay." He started walking out of the pool. "Maybe my mom will buy you one."

By the time Toby got to the lady under the umbrella, she had picked up her purse and was counting out change.

"There's a Coke machine by the door to the ladies' room," she said. "I saw it."

She looked into Toby's eyes and smiled.

All the kids ran to the Coke machine, coins in hand, yelling, "Yeaaa!"

On the way, one of the girls dropped her towel. Toby jumped over it. After they got their Cokes and wandered back, the lady said, "Why don't you all sit in the shade now while you're drinking your Cokes? Relax a minute. That was quite a game!"

"And we're going to play again!" her son announced.

Toby sat cross-legged on the pool deck, drinking his Coke.

The rest of the kids were teasing a girl who never had succeeded in catching anyone during the game.

Toby said to the lady, "Thank you. Thank you for the Coke."

"You're welcome. Are you staying at the motel?"

"Yes, ma'am."

"I haven't seen you before. What's your name?"

"I'm Dink," her son said.

"Toby."

Toby saw a shadow fall over his body. It extended to the shade of the lady's feet.

"Toby Rinaldi."

The lady looked up.

Toby looked around and up.

Standing over him, fists clenched, face red, one eye gleaming furiously, was Spike.

"Get outa here," he said. "Get over there!" He pointed across the pool to his long chair. "Get your towel. You hear me? Get goin'!"

Toby lowered the Coke bottle from his mouth and swallowed.

Clearly, he had done something terribly wrong.

He didn't know what to do with the bottle. It wasn't empty. He shouldn't leave it on the pool deck.

The lady put out her hand. "That's all right. I'll take it. You'd better go with your father."

Toby stood up.

Spike hit him in the back of the head, making him fall forward a step or two, then grabbed him, nearly lifting him off the pool deck, and hurried him along.

Twenty-two

Teddy's voice answering the phone was subdued.

"Teddy! Any news?"

"Not really," he said slowly. "Did you get any sleep?"

"I just keep thinking, Teddy—"

"It's not thinking. It's worrying." His voice fell lower. "It's agony."

"I don't know what—we must—"

"Did Turnbull or any of his henchmen show up there last night?"

"Yes. Colonel Turnbull spent the night sleeping on my couch. He's very nice."

"He didn't strike me as very nice," Teddy said.

"And a couple of men in a yellow Toyota followed me here to the airport. I guess they're his men."

"You're at the airport? In San Francisco?"

"I didn't know what else to do. I came here thinking there just must be some mistake—he got lost, or—"

"There's no mistake, Christina."

"Turnbull belongs to the boss's secret intelligence force, doesn't he?"

Teddy hesitated. "Something like that. Maybe."

"Teddy, you've always known such a thing exists."

"Have I?"

"Well, I have."

"Frankly, Christina, he struck me as sort of vicious."

"Maybe what we need here is 'vicious.' "

"Maybe."

"Oh, Teddy, where is Toby?" Christina held her breath a moment to prevent her crying. "Oh, God, where is Toby? Hasn't there been any word—any ransom demand? Anything?"

There was a long pause before Teddy answered. "No, Christina. There's been no ransom demand."

"Maybe this morning. Most likely this morning," she said. "You'll call the hotel—I mean, the tennis camp— as soon as such a message comes. . . ."

"I'll keep in close touch. Let you know anything we hear. Immediately. . . . What do you think you should do, Christina?"

"I don't know. I guess stay here. At least another twenty-four hours. I keep thinking there must be some terrible mistake. It isn't real. Suddenly Toby will just show up. We don't know what's happening, Teddy. You're there. I should be here. . . . I don't know."

"I don't know, either. I'll call the minute we have any news."

Twenty-three

"I heard you were on your way." Turnbull was sitting on the couch, his feet on the coffee table. On the end table next to him was a bottle of bourbon and a half-empty glass.

"Those men who have been following me all day, do they work for you?" Christina asked.

"For us, dear lady, for us. They are there solely for your protection."

"They—whoever—have got Toby. Why would anyone hurt me?"

"Would you like a drink?"

"No," Christina said. "I'm afraid it would knock me over. Do you have any news for me?"

"Actually, I have." He put his feet on the floor and sat forward. "Not much, but something. Perhaps we should go have dinner. I expect you haven't been treating yourself very well."

"Maybe later." Christina sat in a wicker chair. "Please tell me."

"As I say," Turnbull said, picking up his glass and drinking from it. "Not much. Your little boy's suitcase was found in the airport in New York. Airport maintenance found it in a men's room and brought it to Lost and Found."

"You mean, he's in New York? You know he's in New York?"

"We don't know anything," Turnbull said. "We know his suitcase was found."

Christina swallowed hard. "Makes it sound—I mean, if they dumped his suitcase—as if they didn't expect him to need a change of clothes, or anything. . . ."

"Now, now, Christina. Mustn't think that way." An odd smile came on Turnbull's face. "It might have been left there as a false clue, you know. To make us think Tobias is still in New York."

"Oh, I see." In her lap her fingers were knotted. "I of course, I don't understand much about these things."

"Of course you don't, Christina. Just leave everything to me."

"It's been twenty-four hours," Christina said.

"Yes, and a lot has been done. People have been working on this all night, all day. The suitcase was turned in at two thirty this morning. Our people identified it at six thirty."

She exhaled. "I'm sorry. I can't . . ."

"The other thing I have to tell you is that all flights out of that airport yesterday, all airlines, from noon on, were checked. Children traveling alone, as well as with adults. Mammoth job."

"I'm sure."

"All children flying out of that airport yesterday have been accounted for. Phone calls to the reference numbers established they were who they said they were—except for four. Two couldn't be checked because there was no answer at the phone numbers given. But one of those was a girl and the other a fifteen-year-old boy. One kid was a no-show, but her name was Elizabeth. Another child's phone number must have been given wrong. It didn't exist. But his name was Ling Pao."

Christina was listening intently. "Colonel, why—?"

"I'm trying to show you how thoroughly my people are working, Christina."

"Did they check private airplanes?"

"Yes. Apparently, they can't be as sure who's aboard private aircraft. Just names. . . ."

"So, Colonel, Toby could be on the East Coast, the

West Coast, or anyplace in between. You haven't narrowed it down much."

"Those who kidnapped your child, Christina, have the advantage." The Colonel stared at her solemnly. "They knew they were going to do it. They were able to plan. You and your husband, I must add, did nothing to prevent it."

"Oh . . ."

"I know you haven't much confidence in your Major Mustafa. . . ."

"I am blaming myself," Christina said.

"There, there, Christina." The Colonel's smile was kindly. "Why don't you go change? We'll have a nice dinner."

Twenty-four

"Wandering around the airport all day," Christina said, sitting back in her chair, waiting for her soup, "I felt like one of those shopping bag women, you know? You see them in New York, London. Women with broken shoes, coming from nowhere, going nowhere, going in circles, looking in refuse baskets for God knows what, some evidence of their own existence, some evidence of someone else's existence."

Across from her at the small table in the main dining room of the tennis camp, Colonel Turnbull had his fist firmly around a glass of bourbon and ice.

"What were you looking for?" he asked.

It took her a moment to get her face under control. "Toby."

Colonel Turnbull had prevailed upon her to order a decent dinner: mock turtle soup, a rare steak with salad.

The soup was placed in front of her.

"It seemed a senseless thing to do," Christina said, lifting her spoon. "Wandering around an airport all day. I just didn't know where else to go, what else to do. I couldn't sit by the phone all day. I would have gone completely crazy."

"You just follow your instincts," Colonel Turnbull said. "I have great faith in maternal instincts."

"I have great faith in rationality," Christina said. "And I don't see anything here that makes any sense yet. I called Teddy from the airport—I mean, the Ambassador—"

The Colonel smiled. "You may refer to the Ambassador as Teddy, Christina. I well know who he is."

"He said there had been no ransom demand. No

one had been in touch with him at all about Toby, why he's missing, why they took him."

Across the table, Turnbull allowed his face to become thoughtful, concerned, hesitant.

Christina ate most of her soup before their steaks arrived.

After the waiter left, Colonel Turnbull said, "I'm afraid the Ambassador is being less than frank with you, Christina." As she stared at him, he repeated his point, almost as if enjoying it: "Less than honest."

"There *has* been a ransom demand? Why didn't he tell me?"

"No, not a ransom demand. There's a great deal more at stake here than the mere exchange of money for human life. Doubtlessly, he felt he was sparing you."

Colonel Turnbull shoveled some salad into his mouth.

Chewing, he said, "Your husband received a call last night. From someone who obviously would not identify himself, or for whom he works. We traced the call to a hamburger stand near Baltimore."

"Baltimore? Why Baltimore?"

"Why anyplace? I think the call coming from Baltimore is a pretty good indication of the size of the team we're up against. They're everywhere, nowhere. . . ."

"Are you going to tell me what the man said?"

Colonel Turnbull was now chewing a large piece of steak.

"The man said that if your husband submits Resolution 1176R to the United Nations when he is called upon to do so, your son will be killed."

"Oh." Christina put down her fork. "Oh." She sat back in her chair. "Oh."

"You might as well know everything, Christina. This is the worst kind of political blackmail. You know the flow of oil through the Persian Gulf is slowing down. You know there are people who want the Persian Gulf completely shut. They are willing to go to war over it. His Majesty and your husband drafted this brave little resolution to prevent precisely that happening. It could work." Despite what he was saying, the Colonel appeared to be relishing his dinner. "If your husband gives that speech, your son is dead."

Listening to him, Christina was having a mad rush of thoughts, feelings.

This, too, Toby's kidnapping, has to do with our lives in diplomacy. A little boy who has no more idea of the movement of oil tankers, or concern about it, is kidnapped and facing murder because of the good his father is trying to create. . . .

Why didn't Teddy tell me? I couldn't be worried more or less than I already am. . . .

Oh, yes: when a crisis appears, the nonprofessional, dear-darling-wife Christina, gets shoved aside. . . .

"Poor Teddy," Christina said.

"I'm sure he thought he was being kind—in not telling you."

"He wasn't, you know. Not a bit kind."

"If you're going to help me find Toby," Turnbull said, "I think you should know everything—no matter how difficult for you it is."

"Yes."

"And we must find Toby."

"He could be in New York, in Baltimore—"

"He could be anywhere."

"Colonel, I—I would like to return to the bungalow now. I feel a little woozy. Think I should lie down."

He looked over at her plate. "You didn't eat much, did you?"

"Did the best I could," she said. "Under the circumstances." Christina stood up. "You finish your dinner. I'll be at the bungalow."

*

Augustus Turnbull did finish his dinner.

Christina got up from her bed and went into the living room when she heard him return.

He had just taken off his coat.

He was wearing a shoulder holster. The black metal of the gun gleamed in the weak light of the room.

"Colonel Turnbull," Christina said. "I want to thank you—for being so honest with me."

"Think nothing of it." Turnbull let himself down heavily on the couch and picked up one of the torn magazines. "Can't solve the problem if we don't have all the facts, can we?"

Twenty-five

"Operator? Is this Information operator, New York City? I'm trying to check a phone number."

In a phone booth outside a garage, Spike Mullins had been trying to check a number for more than fifteen minutes. First he dialed the local operator, who gave him the number of local information but did not give him his coin back. He had to get change from the garage. The local Information operator gave him the number to dial for Information New York City. The boulevard traffic outside the phone booth was so noisy he yelled at that operator, who hung up on him.

Now, with the phone booth door closed, Spike was sweating but speaking quietly and hearing fairly clearly.

"The name is Dubrowski," Spike said. "Donny Dubrowski."

"Would you spell that for me, sir?"

"Yeah. Sure. Uh. Du—D-Uah—browski."

"B-R-O-W-S-K-I?"

"Yeah. That's right. Donald. West Eighty-ninth Street, New York City."

"Would that be a new listing, sir?"

"Naw. Donny's been free as a bird seven, eight months now."

The operator recited a number to him. Spike asked her to repeat. She did so while he held the slip of paper up to the phone booth's light. They were the same number.

"Would you try that number for me, operator? It doesn't answer."

"Sir, you may direct dial."

Again the phone went dead.

Standing in the phone booth, glancing over at his rented car, Spike dialed the number three times. He let it ring a dozen times or more each time. Spike could see Toby's head in the passenger seat of the car, watching the cars go by on the boulevard. Finally, Spike hung up, kicked the phone booth's door and returned to the car.

Turning the ignition key, Spike said, "That was your mother, kid. Some delay."

In the dark of the passenger seat, silently Toby was looking at Spike.

"Got to go somewhere else. Wait for her."

Racing the engine, Spike sped back onto the boulevard.

Toby was still looking at him.

"Broke her ankle," Spike said. "Hit a grease spot in the kitchen."

After hustling Toby in from the swimming pool, Spike had scolded him about talking to strangers. Quickly, they had checked out of the Red Star-Silvermine Motel.

They had been driving around ever since, stopping at phone booths.

"Well," Spike said. "Don't blame me! Shit! Ain't my fault your old lady broke her ankle."

After driving awhile again in the dark, they passed a sign saying:

FANTAZYLAND 10

Neither of them said anything.

Twenty-six

Bernard Silvermine stood in the small ballroom of the Ramada Inn. He was wearing a kilt, a brooch and sporran. In his hand was his second scotch and soda.

The piper had not yet come to pipe them to dinner tables across the room. The Highland-dressed people were gathered around the cash bar, catching up on the month's news. For as long as it had existed, twenty-nine years, The Ancient and Honorable Scottish Auxiliary Fusileers—A Charitable Organization had had dinner meetings the second Friday of each month, except June, July, August and September.

Bernard Silvermine had said hello to the hardware man and his wife, asked the price of new faucets; the dentist and his wife, asked about their daughter at U.C.L.A.; the United Parcel delivery man, asked about his wife, forgetting he was recently divorced—and gotten himself a second scotch.

Bernard Silvermine's own wife, sipping her once-a-month gimlet, was standing by the door in a group of everybody's wives except the U.P. delivery man's.

Three men were sitting at the corner of one of the tables. *Good.* One of them was Ed Noakes. Bernard Silvermine wanted to speak to Ed Noakes.

He walked over and sat down.

The three men greeted Bernard Silvermine.

"How's the Red Star-Silvermine Motel working out for you, Bernie?"

"Red Star," said Ed Noakes. "Communist."

"Better than retirement did," Bernard Silvermine said. "Couldn't stand retirement. I recognized I was beginnin' to form opinions about things I knew nothin' about."

"Missus happy?"

"I think so. Hadn't realized it, but she'd sort of been forced into retirement when the kids left home. Least now she doesn't tell me I don't know what I'm talkin' about so much. 'Course I don't have the time to develop great theories about Pakistani politics."

Each of the younger men mentioned his retirement plans. One said he was just going to sit in the sun, and the others—especially Bernard Silvermine—assured him he would do that for three weeks at the most before he found himself wanting to do something else.

"Maybe after thirty years," the man said, "I'll start a garden."

"What're you goin' to do till then?"

"Study up on it."

"Say, Ed," Bernard Silvermine said. "Something I thought I might mention to you."

The other two men didn't hesitate to listen.

"Man and boy checked into the motel yesterday. Rented car. No luggage."

"Jeez, you runnin' that kind of a place now, Bernie?" one of the men asked. "No wonder you can afford a new Buick."

"The boy was no more'n ten years old. He stayed in the car while the man registered. Didn't see the boy until this morning. Registered as Jack Jackson and son, Jack Jackson, Junior."

The expression on Ed Noakes's face didn't change.

"Thing of it is, I don't think they were father and son at all. The man was a real dese-dose-and-dem guy, talked in grunts and groans, you know? And frankly he smelled a little ripe. Looked like an ex-fighter to me, if you know what I mean: face all marked up, glass eye, smashed nose, thick knuckles. Lace burns, the back of his neck. Clothes he was wearing were bought off the rack, and probably outdoors.

"The kid, on the other hand, was wearing a blue

blazer, gray slacks, white shirt, black shoes. His jacket alone probably cost two hundred dollars. And he spoke—his accent was almost English."

Ed Noakes finished his drink.

"This morning the kid said they were waiting for a phone call from his mother. Late this afternoon, way after checkout time, they checked out and left in a hurry. I charged them for an extra night, just to see if the man would give me a story, but he didn't say a word. Paid cash. And they never did get a phone call."

Ed Noakes said, "Did they say where they were goin'?"

"This morning the kid said they were going to Fantazyland. Waiting for his mother, to go to Fantazyland. When I threw him a lot of noise about Jack Jackson and son, Jack Jackson, the kid just looked at me as if I was crazy."

Ed Noakes said, "Anyone for another drink? I do believe I hear the pipes wheezin' up."

"I'll get 'em." The real estate man stood up. "Had a big week last week. Sold a five-story building to a guy who wants to knock it down for a parking lot. Scotch all around? Scotch for you, Bernie?"

"Mine with soda."

The truth was Bernard Silvermine didn't like scotch very much; he also didn't like soda. Too, he always felt a little silly driving through San Francisco and walking into the Ramada Inn in a kilt, brooch and sporran. But The Ancient and Honorable Scottish Auxiliary Fusileers did good, charitable work. Last year they raised all the funds for a new therapy wing of the children's hospital.

And the club was good, too, when you wanted to ask a hardware man informally about the wholesale price of faucets for the motel, or mention something to a Federal Bureau of Investigation agent like Ed Noakes.

Twenty-seven

"I don't know," Teddy said. "My mind keeps closing down. It seems to go to sleep without me. With my eyes open. Suddenly, it's twenty minutes later, a half hour. I forget. . . ."

In Christina's usual place across the breakfast table sat Ria Marti.

Grapefruit halves were before them, but neither was eating.

". . . I forget things. Last night, for the life of me, I couldn't remember the name of the head of the Italian legation. I've known him fifteen years. Can't remember whom I'm supposed to see next, or why. Just now I got a necktie out of the closet, went to the mirror and discovered I already had a tie on. Senile. . . . Too young for this stuff. . . . I just keep seeing Toby's face."

"I think it's called exhaustion," Ria said. "Understandable, justified exhaustion."

"Does one get over it?" he asked innocently.

"You need some time off," she said. "A lot of time off."

"Sounds boring."

"Time doing something else."

"I'd really love to teach for a while now. Put my papers in order, my thoughts. . . . Put my life in order. Some peace and quiet: exciting, stimulating young minds coming to me with urgent questions instead of urgent dispatches. Spend a lot of time with Christina, Toby. . . ."

"Why don't you eat your breakfast?" Ria Marti said.

"I may not be making decisions very well, but it's still my responsibility. I've still got to make 'em."

"Yes, Ambassador."

Twenty-eight

"Are you in the office, Teddy?"

"Yes. Listen, Christina: maybe some real news."

"What?"

It was Saturday morning and Christina was packed and dressed. Colonel Turnbull had left the bungalow before she woke up. She had made a reservation on the one thirty P.M. flight to New York. She was just about to call Teddy when he called her.

It was less than forty-eight hours since Christina had discovered Toby was missing. It seemed an eternity: nothing before that continued to exist with any real clarity; she did not believe this period would ever end.

Packing, she divided this eternity into two periods. At first, in shock, in horror, she had expected all information to come from Teddy. She had waited for him to give her direction. Then she realized there were things she could do, would do—there was a viciousness she could attain to fight this viciousness directed at her child. But she had no fact, no idea, not a scintilla of evidence of any kind to commence with, to direct and guide herself.

Teddy had been less than candid with her. Toby had not been kidnapped for ransom: *"I'm sure he thought he was being kind,"* Colonel Turnbull had said.

Sure, Christina had thought while in the shower washing her hair vigorously. *Little woman. Don't distress her. Save her. Keep her down. Lie to her, or, at least, don't tell her the whole truth. Believe her capable of nothing, don't distress/trust her, keep her in the background. . . .*

On the coffee table in front of her was the note she had written:

"Dear Colonel—Finally slept. This morning I'm still confused, but at least I'm thinking clearer. If I can't accomplish anything here, at least I can be with Teddy. If I have no way of finding Toby, maybe at least Teddy and I should be together through this terrible thing. You have my appreciation for your honesty."

On the telephone, Teddy's voice had slightly more spirit to it.

"There was a message on the F.B.I. telex last night. Just one of a million advisories—"

"I thought we hadn't involved the F.B.I., Teddy."

"Well, ah . . . I guess it was intercepted by our chaps. I guess, ah . . . our chaps had a tap on it. . . ."

There are things Teddy is not willing to tell himself, either—things he's never been willing to tell himself— like the boss's secret intelligence group in this country. He's still not looking straight at that fact, admitting to himself he's been diplomatically dissembling all these years. . . .

"May mean nothing, of course," Teddy continued, "but I'm very hopeful it does mean something. A San Francisco agent reported on the wire last night that a man and a boy checked into a motel called,—let's see, I wrote it down—Red Star-Silvermine Motel. The motel manager got suspicious of them. I guess he didn't believe they were really father and son. The boy was about Toby's age and the manager reported he was dressed expensively, blue blazer, gray slacks, spoke well. He thought the man seemed like kind of a tough guy—a gangster. They registered under the names Jack Jackson and son, Jack Jackson. Of more importance than all that, the description of the man fits the

description Mrs. Brown gave of the man at the airport
here—the man who was supposed to take Toby to the
airplane, Willins. Name of Willins. About thirty, heavy
shoulders, glass eye. All this may mean nothing—"

"Was the boy—was Toby all right?"

Teddy's voice took on a steadying edge. "Christina,
we don't know that it was Toby."

Christina's heart was pounding.

"Are they still at the motel?"

"No. They left hurriedly. Listen to this: the boy told
the motel manager they were waiting for a call from
his mother—who was going to take him to Fantazyland."

"Oh, Teddy." Christina ran her eyes over her suitcases neatly lined up by the bungalow door. "Teddy,
listen carefully, why was Toby's suitcase left in the
men's room in the airport in New York?"

There was a silence before Teddy said, "I'm listening."

"To convince us Toby is still in the New York area.
That, at least, he was taken away from the boarding
gates, back through the terminal—"

"You're saying it was left as a false clue? That therefore Toby was taken from the airport by plane? Christina, we've already checked the airlines, accounted for
every kid on every plane all Thursday afternoon and
night."

"No. There's one plane you didn't check. One last
question—"

"Christina, you know how I am about riddles. At
the moment, I find them especially nerve-wracking."

"Why was Toby's reservation canceled?"

Teddy thought a moment. "That's a good question.
To convince us he wasn't on that plane?"

"Also, Teddy, maybe to make room for someone
who was on that plane. . . ."

"Toby."

"Under another name. Your gnomes didn't check the plane Toby was scheduled to be on, did they?"

"No. I don't think so."

"Would you please ask them to do so?"

"Yes. Of course. I—ah— Where did you get such an idea?"

"Quickly, Teddy. Ask them to check quickly."

"I don't know . . . I don't know that it would help—"

"It would help give some credence that that boy at the Red Silver Mine Motel—"

"Red Star-Silvermine. Silvermine, one word."

"—was Toby."

"Yes," Teddy said. "Colonel Turnbull doesn't believe—"

"Teddy?" Christina pressed the phone closer to her ear. "You knew all along Toby wasn't kidnapped for ransom, didn't you?"

"No," Teddy said. "I didn't know it. But I was pretty sure. The Resolution. . . . Turnbull told me this morning that he's told you the truth about that telephone call . . . threatening Toby's life if I submit the Resolution. Christina, you know there are people who would rather go to war than have me introduce that Resolution Monday night. It's going to cause a complete shift in political alignments—"

"Thanks, Teddy."

"What do you mean?"

"Sorry."

"Look, Christina—"

"I don't know what I mean."

For a long moment, husband and wife listened to each other breathing over long-distance telephone.

Finally, he said, "I'm sorry. Are you staying out there?"

She looked at her suitcases. "Yes."

"I'll call you as soon as I hear anything more," he said.

"Just tell me the truth, Teddy. Please."

Christina placed the telephone receiver in its cradle.

She looked at her suitcases. She looked at the note she had written. She reached out, took the note from the coffee table, crumpled it in her hand and dropped it in a wastebasket.

Twenty-nine

Ria Marti came into the Ambassador's office. Immediately he hung up.

"His Majesty's on the phone," she said. "He asked Sylvia not to break in on you when he understood you were talking with your wife."

"Is he on scrambler?"

"Yes."

Teddy reached for the phone.

"Mr. Ambassador," Ria said. "He's making arrangements to fly to New York."

"Oh?"

"Thought I'd warn you. His being here would make things much more difficult for me. I'd have to explain his sudden arrival." She opened the palms of her hands in a futile gesture. "It would make everything even more impossible than they are for you."

"Yes," Teddy said.

"I'm sure he thinks his being here would be a help. . . ."

Teddy spoke into the phone: "Good morning, Your Majesty."

"Teodoro . . ." The distorted voice was ponderous. "How is Christina?"

"She's handling herself well, sir. Under the circumstances."

"Colonel Turnbull spoke to me a few moments ago from San Francisco, California. His report is not encouraging."

Teddy spoke carefully. "We're slightly encouraged."

"He tells me you received a threatening call which he knows originated in Baltimore, Maryland, that your son's luggage was found in the airport in New York, that there is a highly unreliable report that your son may have been seen in California."

Teddy sighed. His Majesty's ability to cut to the bone often removed hopeful illusions. "That's about it."

Teddy waved Ria Marti out of the room.

"The Colonel tells me he doesn't believe this report of Toby's being at this motel in California—what's it called, the Red Silvermine?—"

"Red Star-Silvermine."

"—is even worth following up. Worth investigating."

"He doesn't? He said that?"

"Yes."

"Then may I ask what the hell is he doing in California?"

". . . Teddy?"

"Sorry."

"I know you're distraught. Are you all right?"

"Yes."

"You can carry on?"

"Your Majesty, this Colonel Augustus Turnbull . . ."

"Yes?"

"He is someone you know personally?"

"I have met with him several times. Of course."

"He is unknown to me."

Teddy had to make that point. Ria had been right: the national news organizations had been on the phone all morning asking for confirmation of the Ambassador's statement that the King did not have a secret intelligence force operating in the United States. Teddy had not spoken with them.

The King simply said, "Yes. He is."

"At this moment, I do not share your confidence in him."

"You are in a position, Teddy, where you have every reason to be critical. Overcritical."

"I'm not sure I'm being overcritical. The other night, questioning me and the staff at the Residence, he struck me as impatient, brusque, abrasive—"

"You can hardly blame him for being impatient, Teddy."

"On occasion, I was convinced that he wasn't even listening. He acted like he knew the answers to questions before he heard them."

"He's a bright man, Teddy. I'm sure the process of questioning people can be tiresome."

"For some reason, I seemed to detect genuine animosity on his part for me."

"He told me." The King paused. "He told me how wrong and . . . irresponsible . . . he thought you were to allow your family to be traveling, especially for pleasure, at such a time as this."

"I admit that," Teddy said. "But I have obligations to my family as well."

"I understand."

"Last night, Turnbull told Christina about the phone call I had received saying that if I offer the Resolution, Toby will be killed. She had been believing this was a matter of kidnap-for-ransom."

"I'm sure the Colonel thought it better she know the truth."

"Frankly, Your Majesty, I think it was uncommonly cruel of him."

"Let's not quarrel with the man's methods just now. He has an impossible job to do, and little time in which to do it."

"I do not have your faith in him."

"But you do have faith in me, Teddy?"

The phone was hurting Teddy's ear. He tried to relax his hand. "Of course."

"Teodoro, I am arranging to come to New York."

"May I ask that you do not do so?"

"I thought I should be with you and your wife—"

"Your Majesty, you cannot submit the Resolution yourself."

"No. I realize that. It would make the Resolution appear far more controversial than it already is. It would extend the debate."

"Also," Teddy said, "it would greatly lessen the chances for the Resolution's being accepted."

"Yes. I understand that. Clearly. And I cannot ask either the Ambassador to the United States or the Ambassador to the Court of Saint James's to substitute for you in submitting the Resolution—"

"That would make the Resolution look like a ploy—something we're just throwing out while really trying to accomplish something else."

His Majesty said, "I'm afraid I'm entirely dependent upon you, Rinaldi."

"Your sudden arrival here would have two negative effects. First, it would direct too much press attention to the Resolution—too many spotlights on the negotiations as they now stand. Other ambassadors would begin grandstanding. I suspect several would vote against us just to strike a tough, popular pose in the world's press."

"I could explain I have arrived suddenly in the United States for medical reasons. Americans are always quick to believe other nations have no doctors."

"Second, Your Majesty, your arrival here would give us the usual intense security problems."

"I'm used to that."

"Pardon me, sir, for being blunt."

"Go ahead."

"You'd be using personnel who instead should be out looking for my son."

There was a long pause. Teddy envisioned His Majesty sitting at his massive desk under the white, fluttering canopy on the terrace, looking out at the Arabian Sea through his dark sunglasses.

"I never thought of that, Teddy. You are quite right. I am delighted to witness that you are thinking clearly."

"May we speak of Turnbull again?"

"Colonel Turnbull? I thought we—"

"No, sir, we haven't. You have arranged matters in such a way that I do not know Colonel Turnbull; I do not know the people he has working for him; I do not know the manner in which he and his people work."

"I thought it wise—"

"It may have been wise. But, at this moment, my ignorance of him is not helpful."

"Again, I fear I must apologize to you."

"No, sir."

"What can I say? Colonel Augustus Turnbull is a native, having been—"

"He is?"

"Yes."

"I thought he was brought up English."

"He was born on a farm near Dahrbahr. His father was a plantation overseer. Didn't your father have a plantation near there, Teddy?"

"I see."

"His father was killed in a farm accident. Augustus and his mother went to England, where he was educated. He joined the British Army, was decorated two or three times and eventually trained in Army Intelligence."

"Oh."

"A rather fine record, as I read it. He came home and joined our Intelligence Service only after a distinguished career with British Intelligence. Of course, it's always so hard to know what these intelligence people actually have done. So much of their lives are closed to us."

"Your Majesty, you consider Augustus Turnbull a loyal subject?"

"Yes. Indeed I do. Why not?"

"Then I request that you apply to him the maximum pressure. Toby must be returned safely to us before the Resolution is submitted Monday night."

There was another long pause. "Mr. Ambassador," the King asked, "are you giving me an ultimatum?"

"I'm requesting that maximum pressure be placed on Augustus Turnbull." Teddy noticed that during this conversation his fingers had shredded the near edge of his blotter. "You see . . ." Teddy swallowed slowly. "We don't have much time. . . ."

"No," His Majesty said, "we don't. Teddy, maximum pressure is being exerted on Augustus Turnbull and his people there. I have complete confidence in him. Give us the weekend."

"We only have the weekend."

"And, Mr. Ambassador? Monday, in the light of facts then prevailing, I will give you a directive. You will follow that directive."

It was not a question.

"Goodbye, Mr. Ambassador."

Thirty

From the motel room not only could Toby hear the music from the carousel, but through the window from almost a mile away he could see Uncle Whimsy's mountain-sized Stovepipe Hat.

He had gotten up and peaked at it through the edge of the window shade at dawn. Somehow he had known it would be there that morning, right in the middle of his window, regardless of whether the window faced north, south, east or west. It had to be there. It was the symbol of Uncle Whimsy, of Fantazyland, which he had seen on comic book covers, in magazines, on television a thousand times.

Toby had known he would get to see Uncle Whimsy's great Hat, as tall as the sky, in reality sometime.

Quietly, he had crawled back into bed. Beyond the shades, the sunlight on the window became brighter and brighter. The air conditioner went on and off. With increasing urgency and frequency, Toby's stomach notified him he was hungry. He told it to be patient and kept still.

Finally, Spike rolled onto his back.

"Ho-hum," said Toby loudly. "Ho-hum."

Spike raised his elbows and rubbed his eyes with his fists.

Toby jumped up, opened the window shades, went into the bathroom, brushed his teeth, showered, dressed in the shorts and sneakers, socks and shirt Spike had bought him the day before, combed his hair somewhat.

When he came out, Spike was sitting on the edge of his bed. He was rolling his glass eye around on the palm of his hand. He carried it with him into the bathroom, tossing it into the air and catching it as he walked.

Toby waited.

First he waited while Spike shaved and then while Spike showered. He waited while Spike dressed. He waited while Spike went to the bureau mirror and popped the glass eye back into his socket.

"Goin' to get a newspaper. You wait here."

"Breakfast," Toby said. "Food. Don't you want your coffee?"

"Dunno about breakfast."

Spike swung the door closed behind him.

And Toby, showered, dressed, ravenously hungry, waited while Spike went to the lobby for a newspaper.

He stood at the window, staring at Uncle Whimsy's Stovepipe Hat standing up like a mountain in the landscape. Its black, cylindrical sides glistened in the morning sunlight. The carousel music was light on the morning air. Occasionally, there was the sound of a man's voice announcing something through a public address system. Toby could not make out the words exactly, but the tone of voice was cheerful. And frequently there was an enormous roar, deeper in tone and louder in volume than any jet engine Toby had ever heard. He tried to envision what sort of a machine would make such a roar. What would it do? Maybe the machine existed simply because of the lovely, awful noise it could make.

It was a temptation for him to sneak out of the motel room, as he did at the Red Star-Silvermine Motel, and get breakfast. The Motel Rancho O'Grady was much bigger, much busier. After Spike had registered the night before, he had returned to the car to get Toby. The only way to their room, Spike had said, was through the lobby. Even at that hour there had been many kids in the lobby, most of them wearing shorts and Uncle Whimsy T-shirts. Spike had hurried Toby through the lobby, even though Toby, too, was wearing shorts and at least no adult had looked at him. A few girls had looked at him; a couple of boys. Toby's T-shirt read, VALVOLINE.

The longer he waited for Spike, the more he wished he had snuck out of the room before Spike had awoken and had breakfast.

But, clearly, today he did not wish to make Spike angry.

When the motel room door opened, Toby turned from the window.

Spike did not have a newspaper in his hand.

Spike's head was so straight he appeared to be looking at Toby with both eyes.

There was the roar of that mysterious machine from Fantazyland.

"Telephones don't work," Spike said. "Fuckin' telephones."

"I'm sorry," Toby said.

Spike sat on the edge of his bed. His shoulders were slumped. His head was low. He was staring at the floor.

"Eggs," Toby said. "Cereal. Bacon. Sausage. Orange juice. Toast. Coffee for you."

Spike said absently, "What? What're you talkin' about?"

"Breakfast!" Toby said. "A little thing called breakfast! Breakfast is next!"

"Oh, yeah." Spike reached for the phone between the unmade beds. "Sure, kid. I'll call up. We'll have it here."

*

Spike sent Toby to the bathroom while breakfast was being laid out in their room.

Toby popped out of the bathroom and sat down at the portable table as soon as he heard the door close.

Spike had repeated into the telephone everything Toby had said. And there everything was jammed on the table: eggs, cereal, bacon, sausage, orange juice, toast and coffee.

Toby began eating everything at once.

Spike was slow to sit down. He drank a cup of coffee before he touched any food.

Toby thought Spike was looking, sounding, acting like his math teacher the mornings he smelled of whiskey and the other kids said he had a hangover. Spike was moving slowly, not saying much. His face looked like he would be glad to burp. Even his real eye was slightly glassy. He did not smell of whiskey, though.

After Spike began eating, Toby said, "Spike? If you wanted to hide a shoe, where would you hide it?"

"What?"

"Simple question: where would you hide a shoe?"

"Stupid question."

"Sensible question. Where would you hide a shoe?"

"Another one of your stories about damn fools who fly through the air in their pajamas?"

"Where would you hide a shoe?"

Spike blinked around the room. "Under the bed."

"Why under the bed?"

"No one would see it there."

"They would, if they were looking for the shoe?"

"Why would anybody be looking for the shoe?"

"Are there many shoes under the bed?"

"I dunno. I haven't looked. Could be corpses, for all I know." Spike stabbed his scrambled eggs. "Why are you talking this way? I didn't take your shoe. Dumb kid."

"Ask me where I'd hide a shoe—if I had to hide a shoe."

"In a closet."

Toby shook his head. "First place anyone would look for a shoe. That's where a shoe's supposed to be."

"It is? I never put no shoes in no closets."

"Ask me."

"Ask you what, for Chrissake?"

"If I had to hide a shoe," Toby said, "I'd hide it in a shoe store."

"Oh, yeah." Spike chewed thoughtfully. "Like hidin' a needle in a haystack."

"No," said Toby. "Like hiding a piece of hay in a haystack. I'd hide a needle in a sewing box."

"But a needle's supposed to be in a sewing box."

"Yeah. But no one would expect you to *hide* a needle in a sewing box."

Toby munched awhile, then said, "Spike, where would you hide a speck of sand?"

"Anywhere."

"A speck of sand you know other people are looking for."

"Why would anyone look for a speck of sand?"

"You'd hide in on the beach."

"I would not."

"Why not?"

"I'd never find it again."

"That's true," Toby said.

They ate in silence for a while.

Toby said, "Are we going to stay in this room all day?"

"Why?"

"I noticed you made me go into the bathroom when the man brought breakfast to us."

"Oh. Fac' is, you needed to go to the bathroom, anyway."

Toby ate another piece of toast.

He then said, "I guess when people tell you and me to stay in a room, Spike, we have to do it. Right, Spike?"

Spike looked annoyed. "It's the telephone. Can't get nobody to answer the telephone."

Faintly, they could hear the carousel music from Fantazyland.

"Spike?"

"Why don't you stifle it? Punk kid."

"If you had to hide a kid, where would you hide him?"

Spike glanced at the bathroom door.

Then he stared at Toby.

Toby said, "I think a school yard would be a pretty good place to hide a kid."

Spike continued to stare at him.

"Don't you think a school yard would be a pretty good place to hide a kid?"

"Yeah, kid. Sure. A school yard would be a fine place to hide a kid."

He poured himself some more coffee.

Toby said, "Anywhere there are lots of other kids."

Again, Fantazyland's mysterious machine roared.

Toby continued to look at Spike. The man's fists were clenched tight. He was looking over his shoulder at the window, through the window, maybe seeing the top of Uncle Whimsy's Hat.

Spike picked up his coffee cup and took it to the window. His back was to Toby.

After a moment, very cheerfully, Toby said, "Hey, Spike! We goin' to Fantazyland now? Nice day for it. . . ."

Spike drained his coffee cup before turning around.

"Fac' is," he said, "we are."

He left the coffee cup on the bureau and picked up the car keys.

"Fac' is, I'm sick of your conversation."

Thirty-one

The old man in short pants, standing on a ladder puttying in a window, didn't see her.

"Good afternoon," Christina said.

The man looked down. "Hi."

"You're Mr. Silvermine?"

"Always have been," the man said.

"The person in the motel office said I might find you here."

"Well. You have."

Christina opened her wallet and handed it up to him.

He squinted at it, took it in his hand, held it out of the sunlight. Then he looked at her.

"Oh. You his mother?"

"Yes. Do you recognize him?"

"Sure do." He handed the wallet back to her and, leaving his tools on top of the step ladder, climbed down. "Thought I hadn't heard the end of this."

The man was looking carefully at her. "That man. Traveling with the boy. Your son. Jackson. Not the boy's father, was he? Your husband?"

"No."

"Thought not." He shook his head, blinked. "This is the quietest kidnapping I've ever heard of—now that I know it's a kidnapping. 'Spose there's a reason for it? I mean, you all being so quiet about it."

"Yes."

"But the F.B.I. must be involved," Mr. Silvermine said. "Ed Noakes is the only one I spoke to about it."

"No," said Christina. "They're not."

"Come on. Let's go into the office. Get out of this sun, even though, like me, it's past its prime."

Walking with him across the patch of lawn, Christina said, "I just wonder if there's anything you can tell me. Anything. For example, by any chance do you have the registration of the car?"

"Sure do. Didn't give it to Ed Noakes 'cause I had just the faintest suspicion that I was bein' a busybody. Not my role in life to harass people if they don't need harassin'. Enough people have taken on that role for themselves."

In the office, he copied down the registration of the car on a slip of paper and handed it to her. "Not sure that will do you any good. Pretty sure it's a rented car. People change cars these days faster than they change facial expressions. All the cars look alike, anyway, whether they call 'em Chryslers or Oldsmobiles. All the facial expressions look alike, too, come to think of it. Orthodontisized grills up front, ears you can't see. Teeth everywhere you look. How about some iced tea?"

"Love it."

"Let's go into the dining room and see if anybody workin' for me is workin' for me."

*

At the table, over tall glasses of iced tea, Mr. Silvermine leaned forward and said, "Arrived Thursday night. Man came in to register, boy stayed in car. That's unusual. Little kids usually like to come in with their fathers, 'specially boys. If they're awake. Saw his head through the window, stickin' up over the dashboard. Wide awake. Didn't really lay eyes on your little boy till next morning, real early. As soon as the dining room opened for breakfast, he presented himself in the lobby, enlisting my authority to permit him to order breakfast. I was taken by the way he was dressed—black shoes, gray slacks, white shirt, blue blazer. Even the president of the United States wouldn't be dressed that way in the lobby of a motel at seven o'clock in the morning, if he had other clothes. Struck me that if the boy had any other clothes, shorts or jeans or somethin', he'd be wearin' 'em. Then I perceived he was a well-spoken child, and the man who registered as his father had given me the distinct impression he believed vocabulary was something meant for other people. I guess I was a little suspicious. I threw a quick routine at him about his name, Jack Jackson, son of Jack Jackson, and although he didn't answer me, he also didn't particularly seem to know what I was talking about."

"How did he seem to you?"

"Right as rain. Hungry. Mostly anxious about his breakfast."

"He wasn't wounded in any way?"

"No. Not at all. I saw him later playing in the swimming pool. No bruises as far as I could see."

"He was playing in the swimming pool?"

"Later. Later in the afternoon."

"Was this man, Jackson, with him at that time?"

"Yup. He was sittin' to the side, dozin'."

"This is hard for me to understand," Christina said. "I've been envisioning . . . gagged, tied in a closet, beat up."

"I'm sure you have. None of that was goin' on, as far as I could see." Bernard Silvermine thought a minute. "'Course, it would be pretty hard to move a child around in that condition, bound and gagged. You'd sort of have to keep him in one place, if you know what I mean. Lose your freedom of movement."

"But how are they doing it? What have they told him?"

"Oldest story in the world," Bernard Silvermine said. "Get a child to come along with you by the promise of candy. Con him. Make him think if he comes along nicely, he'll get somethin' he wants. Isn't that always the story?"

Christina had not touched her iced tea. "Tell me about this man. Jackson."

"Not terribly tall, but heavily, I mean, powerfully built. Big shoulders, chest, thick arms and neck. Glass eye. His face was pretty well cut up."

"What do you mean, 'cut up'? Acne? Chicken pox? Knife scars?"

"Very distinctive scars. Follow the fights somewhat, you know. Always fascinates me how one man can make a business out of knockin' other men senseless."

"I don't get you."

"He had the scars of a fighter. A professional fighter. Scars over his eyes, mashed nose, lace cuts the back of his neck."

"A fighter."

"Boxer. Retired boxer."

"Why do you say 'retired'? Because of his age?"

"No. He wasn't that old. Didn't I say he had a glass eye? Can't fight with a blind side. Have to be able to see out of both sides of your head.",

"He sounds pretty ugly."

"Well, I doubt he'd ever be taken up as a model for aftershave."

"But what kind of a person did he seem like? I know that's a stupid question. . . .'"

Bernard Silvermine looked at her a long moment before answering. "Frankly, he seemed a pretty tough character. But don't take that too much to heart. I'm older than you, by a day or two, and I can tell you I've never met a person yet who is what he looks like. People with wide open, innocent faces seem to have more latitude in bein' rotten. I find that people who are born lookin' rotten already seem to have to toe the line a little closer. All I can say is your boy seemed all right when I saw him."

"Any idea where they went?"

"No, ma'am. People aren't apt to leave forwardin' addresses at a motel. The home address Jackson signed was 200 Park Avenue, Saint Louis, Kentucky. The imponderability of all that didn't strike me until later. Paid cash. No credit card. The boy—your son— told me he was goin' to Fantazyland—which might have been the candy Jackson was usin' to keep him in line. Then again, the boy also told me he was waitin' on a call from his mother—you. You were comin' to take him to Fantazyland."

Christina's eyes roamed around the empty dining room.

Bernard Silvermine waited patiently, to hear if she had any other questions.

Finally, he said, "California's just one big parking lot, you know—strips of it movin'."

"What do you mean?"

"Even highway patrol doesn't seem to be able to find any particular car too quickly."

"No," she said. "I don't suppose so."

"I don't know what to tell you," Bernard Silvermine said. "Anything at all I can do to help?"

"No." Christina took her handbag off the table and stood up. "Really, I'm very grateful to you. This is the first real lead we've had."

Bernard Silvermine said, "Delighted to hear I'm not a busybody. Not that I was losin' any sleep over the possibility."

He had risen and she had put her hand in his. "Thank you so very much, Mr. Silvermine."

"I have a question. Busybody question. What's your son's name?"

"Toby."

"That's a right nice name," Bernard Silvermine said. "Right nice. You know, I wouldn't mind too much knowin' where there's good news."

"What? Yes. Of course."

"Otherwise, I won't want to know, if you understand me."

"Yes."

"I'd rather think maybe you just forgot to tell me."

"I understand," Christina said. ". . . I understand."

Thirty-two

The parking lot at Fantazyland was the largest Toby had ever seen. They had to follow the hand signals of six people before they were parked properly.

And Uncle Whimsy's Stovepipe Hat rose up into the sky from the nearby landscape higher than Toby had ever dared think possible. He could see the little gondolas, bright red, yellow, green, pop out of the hole near the Top of The Hat, the people in them barely distinguishable, zip around a curve, vanish into another hole in The Hat, reappear from a tunnel a little further down, climb slowly, plunge down into another tunnel.

They had to walk a long way through the sun-dazzled parking lot to get to Fantazyland's main gate. And then wait in line for tickets.

UNCLE WHIMSY WELCOMES YOU—ONE AND ALL—TO FANTAZYLAND. Toby read the sign a million times. He had known, really known, that someday he would get to read that sign.

If you need help at Fantazyland, ask your Constable. Emergency medical facilities are available near main gate.

Spike bought two books of tickets, good for two days' admission, a ticket for every ride.

Inside the main gate, constables stood around, men in blue suits, wide belts, truncheons hanging from them, handlebar mustaches and helmets.

A giant Uncle Whimsy, stovepipe hat, bright pink face with white-painted smile and smiling eyes, baggy pants and three-foot-long high-button shoes, greeted them. His gloved hand on Toby's head was so big and floppy it fell over Toby's shoulders.

Spike's hand disappeared in Uncle Whimsy's glove.
"Glad to meetcha, glad to meetcha," Spike said.
"You're a big bastid, arncha?"

A nearby constable gave Spike a sharp look.

And Uncle Whimsy moved away.

Immediately inside the main gate, they were in the
square of a town that had never existed, except in
people's longings.

In the middle of a green, four-squared park was a
bandstand on which mustached firemen played trum-
pets and saxophones and an oboe and drums, *When
the Saints come marchin' in.* . . . Horse-drawn car-
riages went around the square and up and down the
main street. One horse relieved itself and instantly a
man in a white suit was there with shovel and broom
and a barrel on wheels to clean it up.

On one side of the square was a Fire Station, its
doors open. Inside was a horse-drawn pumper and an
antique fire truck, kids swarming over both, ringing
the bells. Next to it was a Candy Store (the biggest
store in the square).

Also on the square was an Emporium, a Mercantile
Establishment, a Newspaper Office (*People with press
passes please check in here*), a Drug Store (*Ice
Cream, Notions & Sundries*), a small Lawyer's Office,
a large Doctor's Office with a Red Cross flag outside
(*Doctor Is In—for medical emergencies*), a Chamber
of Commerce Office (*Special Guests of Fantazyland,
please check in here*), a movie theater (*See Charlie
Chaplin! Harold Lloyd! Abbott & Costello!*) and a
Sandwich Shoppe. Poles atop the buildings flew the
flags of all nations, although Toby could not find the
flag of his nation.

"Jeez," Spike said, standing, staring. "Just like Newark."

First they went to the Candy Store, where Spike
bought a bag of peppermints ("Good for your

breath") and Toby a bag of licorice ("That stuff shits," Spike said.)

Munching, they listened to the band music for a while. Spike hummed along with such a dreadful voice the space around them cleared. Then they ambled around the square. Going by the Fire Station, Toby looked in and guessed it wouldn't take him all that long to work his way through the crowd of kids, take his turn in the drivers' seats and ring the fire bells.

Spike said, "Kids' stuff. Ya see, that's kids' stuff."

Continuing to look around doors, Toby noticed that although the dresses in the windows of the Emporium had hoops and hobbles and bustles and veils for sale at low, low prices, inside the store were jeans and T-shirts and shorts with no prices visible.

At the end of the street was a signpost with three arrows. The one pointing right said, TO THE FUTURE; to the left, TO THE PAST; straight ahead, THRILLS, CHILLS AND SPILLS.

Toby wanted to go straight ahead. He knew that path led to Uncle Whimsy's Hat.

Spike said they would go to the left.

On the main street of Wild West City stood a man dressed in black cowboy gear, snarling at the people, cracking a bullwhip. He wore a black patch over one eye.

"Look at that turkey," Spike said.

They tried their luck in a shooting gallery. Toby's score was twelve hits out of twenty shots. He was awarded an Uncle Whimsy Comic Book. Spike's score was seven.

"Rigged," Spike said. "Can't trust nobody. Bastids."

Walking along, Spike said, "I ain't tol' you 'bout the time I shot this guy. . . . He was up on a roof in Newark, eight, nine storys high. I was in the street, block away. Single shot with my pistol, from my hip.

That was a real gun, none of this shooting-gallery crap. Fac' is. . . ."

The cracks of the bullwhip became sharper, more frequent, more insistent. A cowboy dressed in white came out of The Marshal's Office. He and the villain glared at each other. The marshal stepped into the street. The villain dropped his whip. They circled around each other. The large semicircle of tourists, dressed in bright shirts and shorts, grew six deep.

The two cowboys drew on each other and fired. For a moment, each stood there. Then a red stain appeared on the villain's shirt, over the heart, and he fell forward, biting the dust.

The tourists smiled and laughed and applauded and took pictures.

Four other cowboys appeared, picked the villain up by his hands and feet and carried him off.

"Make believe," Spike said. "Fac' is, it ain't real, ya know. None of this stuff."

There was a Wild West Clothing Store—more jeans, shorts and Uncle Whimsy T-shirts, ten-gallon hats and big belt buckles—a Dance Hall Saloon with a list of prices outside for fruit juices, soft drinks. Toby heard a piano tinkling. Two or three heavily made-up women, hair piled on top of their heads, gowns cut low, stood outside, saying to the men, "Hiya, honey. . . ."

Spike reached into the skirt of one and pinched her bottom.

"Hiya, honey," he said. "Whatcha doin' after the show?"

At first the woman looked shocked, then disgusted; then she looked away.

In various places, when they were just standing there looking around, Toby heard the hum of machinery. He didn't ask if Spike heard it too. He noticed little booths here and there (in the village by the main gate they were old-fashioned telephone booths, without windows; in the Wild West village they were outhouses)—all marked *Employees Only*. Especially standing near these booths, he heard the humming noises. He thought the sounds nearest the booths sounded like elevators.

There was a corral with live ponies, one of which Toby rode; another area of mechanical horses, bucking broncos, which they both rode. The mechanical horses were more lively than the live.

They were in Wild West City so long the villain reappeared in the street, with a fresh black shirt, again cracking his whip at people.

"Turkey," Spike said.

Over the tuna sandwiches at an outdoor pavilion, they studied their ticket books and discussed where they'd go next. Toby pressed for THRILLS, CHILLS AND SPILLS, but Spike said he thought THE FUTURE would be more interesting. Near them was a seven-foot-tall white stem of a ship's air vent. At the beginning of lunch, Toby saw a constable step up to the vent, open a door in it with a key, step inside and close the door. Toby kept careful watch all through lunch. The constable never came back out of the vent. However, near the end of lunch, the door in the vent opened again and out stepped a woman in a space suit, carrying her helmet.

Everywhere they had gone in the park, people dressed as constables, clowns, bears, space travelers, rabbits, shook hands with people, patted children's heads, held babies, struck silly poses with tourists while having their pictures taken. While they were finishing up their sandwiches, a fountain in the middle of the pavilion rose up slowly. Music became louder and louder. Under the fountain rose a stage. On it, a band with electric guitars and drums played; four girls, all blondes in slinky red dresses, sang. *Why don't you love me, baby? I can bake a cake . . .*

Spike turned around. "Where'd they come from?"

"Look, Spike." Toby pointed up in the air. "The fountain's still working! Over their heads!"

"Well, I'll be a goose's rear door!"

That afternoon they visited THE FUTURE: circled a lake in a ship that traveled on an air cushion, its engines making the lovely, awful noise Toby had heard from the motel; visited the bottom of the lake in a submarine, stared through the portholes at simulated ocean growths and fish; whipped around the lake on a Future Bus that also traveled on an air cushion, making a ground noise; talked into telephones that permitted them to hear Japanese ("What's that shit?" Spike said as he listened. "Not me!"); blasted off in a space ship, rushed through the atmosphere, watching the world become smaller behind them, then burst into the galaxy and floated among the stars to tinkling music.

"Whaddaya think of this?" Spike asked himself out loud.

"Inneresting," he answered. "Inneresting."

They also visited the Spooky House. Eyeballs of portraits followed them; ghosts walked by them in the dark, moaning. Chains rattled. The room lurched, suddenly changing dimensions. Headless ladies and gentlemen appeared, dancing a minuet.

And The Pirate's Caravelle. Gold spilled from a chest on the lower deck. Sailors languished in the brig. On the upper deck a sailor, dressed only in torn-off pants and a blindfold, hands tied tightly behind his back, was forced to walk the plank.

The tourists smiled and laughed and applauded and took pictures.

Spike and Toby watched a long time, but the man never rose to the surface of the water.

"Poor dude," Spike said. "He croaked."

They went in a dugout through The Dangerous Swamp. Mechanical alligators and crocodiles came to the edge of the boat and snapped their teeth at them. The dugout veered away. Along the embankment, ten-foot mechanical bears waved them nearer and roared at them. Huge snakes slithered down the trees. On a little island they passed, there was a log cabin burning.

"Fantastic!" Spike said, "fac' is, you know, all this is fake, you know. I mean, that cabin isn't really burnin'. It's takin' too long. It just looks like it's burnin'."

They were walking across an old wooden bridge. It began to tremor. It wobbled. It lurched down to the left. They could see and hear the timber supports breaking. Three sharks appeared across the lagoon and came at them with horrendous speed. One after the other, they came to the edge of the bridge, their mouths open, reaching for them. . . .

"Jeez," said Spike, drawing back. "Getcha to believe it."

Toby knew they were coming to the base of Uncle Whimsy's Stovepipe Hat.

But down a path, Spike saw a great, smooth cement bowl in the landscape. In it, people were driving brightly painted, rubber-wheeled, rubber-bumpered cars, gathering speed, smashing into each other, laughing, bouncing off.

"I gotta try that!" Spike said.

Spike hustled into the driver's seat.

"Hey, Spike! I'm drivin'!"

"Bullshit you are, kid. You're too young."

"Other kids my size are driving!"

Spike looked around. "Oh, yeah. So they are. Next time. Next time you get to drive."

Spike drove. He gave himself the maximum space

to gather the maximum momentum to crash into people with the maximum force.

"Hyaaa! Gotcha, ya bastids!"

Some of his victims looked offended.

Spike gave them the raspberry.

When Toby drove, it took him a while to discover how the pedal and steering wheel worked.

"Go get those dudes!" Spike shouted. Toby was nudging other cars gently. "Smash 'em! Smash 'em!"

A plaid car came from nowhere and hit them so hard their car rocked sideways.

"Why, you bastids!" Spike tried to stand up in the car to get out. He shook his fist at them. "Let me outa here! I'll kill the bastids!"

Toby started the car with a jerk and Spike fell back into his seat.

"Ah, dumb kid," Spike said when the ride was over. "Whaddaya you know? Nothin'! Nothin' at all. All you think life is is fun fun fun fun."

Ultimately, they came to the line at the base of Uncle Whimsy's Hat.

Spike put his hands on his hips, leaned back and stared up at the top. Directly over them, on little tracks, the gondolas were zooming in and out of The Hat, down the sides.

"Jeez, kid. Look at that."

"Let's get in line, Spike."

Spike waggled his head. "Not safe."

"Whaddaya mean, 'not safe'? Spike, it's been working for years!"

"Not safe," Spike said.

Quietly, Toby said, "Chicken."

Spike took a step toward him. "Whad you say?"

"Cluck-cluck-cluck," Toby said. "Chicken!"

"Don' you never say nothin' like that to me!"

"All right, then. Let's get in line."

"No."

"CLUCK-CLUCK-CLUCK!"

"Dumb kid, whadda you know?"

"I know you're a chicken."

Spike looked at the ground, at the people waiting in line to go on the ride down Uncle Whimsy's Hat. He looked at the ground again.

"Cluck," Toby said.

Spike broke into the head of the line, pushing people aside. Toby stayed right with him.

❋

The shadows were longer.

Spike sat on a cement bench. His face was ashen. His lips were slack. His hands were shaking.

Toby stood on the sidewalk, facing him.

"Have I still got my eye?" Spike felt for it with his fingers.

"Yeah."

On the ride coming down The Hat, through The Hat, down, down, plunging through black tunnels, roaring out into sunlit space, twirling around in midair, down, down, rushing down, Spike sat, back straight, clutching the safety bar with both hands. His mouth was open, his neck muscles strained.

He was bellowing, "Oh—hhhhhhhh!"

Laughing, Toby joined him. "Ah—hhhhhhh!"

Going through the pitch-black tunnels, Toby had the impression Spike's head was a white balloon on a string being towed along beside him.

It wasn't until the little gondola slowed down, near the bottom, that Toby realized Spike wasn't having fun.

Spike wanted to get out of the gondola immediately. He saw the platform, but his movements were uncertain. His knees wobbled.

Spike was a shaken man. He went to the nearest bench and sat down.

"That's enough for today, kid," he finally said. "This place gives me the creeps. Hard to remember nothin's real, ya know?"

He stood up, putting his hand on the back of Toby's neck.

"Let's go back to the motel now."

"We can come back tomorrow, though. Right, Spike?"

"Sure, sure," Spike said.

"There's lots we haven't seen yet."

"Yeah," Spike said as they walked along. "The Wax Museum. The Duck Pond. Princess Daphne's Flower Castle. . . ."

Thirty-three

Bernard Silvermine saw the green four-door sedan pull into the parking lot in front of the Red Star-Silvermine Motel and park immediately in front of the main door, where there was a sign saying, NO PARK-ING—LOADING AREA.

A heavy man rolled out of the driver's seat, slammed the door and stood a moment looking at the motel. He wore a rumpled green tweed suit. Before he adjusted his jacket there was a noticeable bulge under his left shoulder.

When the man stood at the reception counter, Bernard Silvermine looked up at him inquiringly, but said nothing.

The man put a school photo of Toby on the counter. Bernard noticed that in laying the picture on the counter, the man had his thumb on Toby's face.

"Ever seen that child before?" the man asked.

Bernard Silvermine looked at the sweaty thumb-print. "Who are you?"

The man's tone was official, if not authoritative. "You, or someone else at this motel, reported to the Federal Bureau of Investigation your suspicion that a boy staying at this motel the night before last in the company of an unidentified man was the victim of kidnap."

"Are you with the F.B.I.?" Bernard Silvermine asked mildly.

The man's small eyes were impudent, Bernard Silvermine thought. "How else would I know you reported it?"

"That I don't know," Bernard Silvermine said. "But I know you're not with the F.B.I."

"I'm with a private police agency," the man said. His hand went to his back pocket.

"That's all right," Bernard Silvermine said. "There's no need to show me credentials." He picked up Toby's picture, held it in the light of the plate-glass windows, shook his head and said, "That's not the boy, anyway."

"It's not?"

Bernard Silvermine put the photograph back on the counter.

"No, indeed," he said. "The boy who was here had red hair and freckles."

The man took the picture off the counter. He hesitated before putting it back in his pocket. He appeared to have more questions for Bernard Silvermine, but didn't seem immediately sure what they were.

"I wonder," Bernard Silvermine said, "if you'd be good enough to remove your car from my loading zone?"

Outside, a chambermaid was trying to get her laundry wagon by the green sedan.

Bernard Silvermine said, "I mean, like move it. Now."

He watched the heavy man cross the lobby, push through the glass door and, with deliberate slowness, get into the car and start it while the chambermaid waited in the hot sun.

I wonder if Toby's mother knows, Bernard Silvermine thought, *that someone else is looking for her son—and that that someone is no particular friend.*

Thirty-four

"I wonder if you could help me," Christina said to the young woman behind the car rental counter at San Francisco Airport. "I'm Mrs. Cummings. I live in Los Altos Hills. . . ."

Christina had given the same story to the other two car rental agencies at the airport and drawn a blank.

She held the piece of paper Bernard Silvermine had given her with the registration number written on it.

". . . Do you ride bicycles?" she suddenly asked the young woman behind the counter.

"Yes, I do," the young woman said. "My husband races."

The two women smiled at each other at the thought of a representative of a car rental agency riding a bicycle.

"My son has a very precious bicycle," Christina said. "He paid for it himself. A Motobecane Gran Record."

There was clear recognition in the young woman's face. "That's a hell of a bike," she said.

"Not inexpensive," Christina agreed.

"Does your son race? I mean, your son must be pretty young."

"I think he means to try," Christina said. *Oh, my. Don't they make Motobecane Gran Records for youngsters?* She had first seen one only the previous week. Her pro at the All Stars' Tennis Camp had one. *This person knows bicycles. Have I made a mistake?* "Actually, he's my husband's son," Christina said. "He's seventeen."

"Oh. I was wondering. That's a professional kind of bike for a kid. I mean, a little kid."

Christina nodded. "It's a very good bike. Anyway, he had it with him at the ball field the other night, and a car hit it. Squished it."

The young woman's face fell.

Christina assured her, "My son wasn't on it. The bicycle was just on the grass, you see. . . ."

The young woman's face didn't seem relieved. *My God. This person is struck dumb by the tragedy of a bike's being run over.*

"Anyway"—Christina held up the piece of paper— "my neighbor-friend, Mrs. Scalise, took down the registration number of the car that ran over the bike and gave it to me. See? 7NP 4484. And she said she thought she saw one of those car-rental stickers near the back bumper. I'm just wondering if the car belongs to your agency, and if possibly you could give me the name and address of whoever rented the car from you?"

The young woman had read the registration number. She said, "We're not liable for accidents—"

"Oh, no," Christina said quickly, "I'm not thinking that. I'm just thinking that I'd write to the person who squished the bike—"

"He might have insurance," the girl said. "Well, he ought to have insurance."

"Yes," Christina said.

"But I don't want the agency held responsible."

"Of course not," Christina said. "But don't you think someone who squished a bike should be told he had done so? Especially a Motobecane Gran Record?"

The young woman nodded firmly. "Especially a Motobecane Gran Record."

"At least," Christina said, "he ought to be told what it was he squished."

"Indeed, yes." The young woman took the paper. "I'll find out what I can."

While the young woman was going through her

agency records, Christina turned her back to the counter and looked at the airport.

Such an odd mix of sights and sounds. There were little people with big suitcases, big people with little cases; people dressed in three-piece suits, people dressed in cut-offs and jerseys; people hurrying madly, people standing looking bored out of full consciousness. The general sounds were cavernous; the public address announcements penetrating; the occasional whine and roar of the jets taking off and landing oddly suppressed.

Airports had always been happy places for Christina. She had met Teddy for the first time at an airport. She recalled the days flying back and forth from New York and college to spend weekends with him. Later, after they were married, flying from London to Geneva, New York to St. Croix for vacations . . . flying in His Majesty's private jet.

She wasn't sure she'd ever like airports again. An airport, this airport, was where Toby hadn't shown up when he was supposed to. *Perhaps I'm obsessed by this airport*, she thought. *I keep coming back to it. In this airport, there has to be a lead, somewhere, somehow.*

"Mrs. Cummings?"

Christina turned around. The young woman had a long, yellow piece of paper in her hand.

"That car was rented by a Charles Mullins, a driver licensed by the state of New Jersey."

She handed Christina back the small piece of paper that had the registration number on it. "Here, I wrote down his name and home address for you."

Christina looked at the paper, feigning great interest in it. She still did not know what she wanted to know.

"Tell me," Christina said easily. "Has the man turned the car back in yet?"

The young woman looked at her curiously.

"What I mean is," Christina said, "there's no hurry in writing him if we know he hasn't gone home yet."

"Oh." The young woman consulted her piece of paper. "No. It's an open-ended return."

"He has not returned the car?"

"No. If he had, the computer would have marked it available."

"I can't thank you enough," Christina said. "It's a small matter, of course, but my son—"

The young woman flipped her index finger at Christina. "Squishing a good bike is no small matter."

Thirty-five

Christina ran the last few meters down Slave Alley in the dusk. She'd heard the phone ringing in the bungalow.

Once inside the bungalow, she instantly picked up the receiver.

"Hello?"

The reading lamp near the telephone was on.

"Christina? Good guess."

"Teddy, listen—"

"You were right about the flight Toby was supposed to be on. In fact, it looks like he was on it. There was a last-minute reservation for a man and a boy. Reservation in the name of Doland. Major Mustafa found one of the stewardesses who had served that flight and spoke to her by phone. Caught her between flights in Toronto. She remembers the man because, well, she saw him do something unusual to the boy, and—"

"What do you mean, 'do something unusual to the boy'? Teddy, what did he do to Toby?"

"Nothing, really. It's all right. A small thing."

"Teddy, you'd better tell me what the stewardess saw the man do to Toby!"

"He twisted Toby's fingers. Bent them back. Apparently to make him shut up. A childish thing, really."

"Was Toby all right? It must have hurt him."

"Well, Christina, this whole—"

"Oh, Teddy."

"Anyway, he fits the description Mrs. Brown gave us of the guy at the airport. The stewardess remembers his glass eye. And her description of the boy pretty well fits Toby—age, coloring, dress."

"Teddy, listen. Toby is here."

"What?"

"No, I'm sorry. Not here. I mean, on the West Coast. The man at the motel, the Red Star-Silvermine Motel, identified Toby from that little picture I keep in my wallet."

"Positively?"

"No doubt at all. Toby was there two nights ago. Again, the same description of the man with Toby. Mr. Silvermine thinks the man may have been a boxer."

"Did he have any idea where they might have gone?"

"None. But I have the registration number of the car they were driving."

Teddy thought before speaking. "Give it to Colonel Turnbull."

"I checked it out as much as I could. The car is rented to a Charles Mullins, of New Jersey."

Teddy's voice was becoming increasingly thoughtful. "I don't think the name means anything, Christina. How many names has he used so far? Willins, Doland, Jackson—"

"Teddy, the important thing is that the car hasn't been returned to the rental agency yet. That means they're still somewhere in this area." Teddy did not say anything. "Here in the San Francisco Bay area."

Finally Teddy said, "I guess that narrows it down somewhat."

"Only somewhat," she said. "But before we had the whole world to search! And now we have the car registration number." Again, Teddy was saying nothing. "What do I do now?" Christina asked.

"Give any information you have to Colonel Turnbull."

"Yes. All right. I will."

"The boss has complete faith in him." Teddy was

now using the voice he used in giving directives late at night: low, tired, efficient. "By the way, Christina, His Majesty is being totally supportive."

"Does he still say you have to give that speech?"

Teddy's voice became lower, tireder, more efficient. "There is no doubt in his mind about that, Christina."

Still standing, facing the side wall of the living room, Christina realized she was staring at a film-star poster on the wall. Seen from this short distance, the girl's bathing suit was transparent.

"Teddy? I don't mean to add to your burdens, right now, and that's not why I'm saying this. . . ."

"Saying what?"

"After we get Toby back . . . What I mean is . . . we have to find some other way of life. . . . I mean, if we're going to live together. . . . Teddy? Are you there?"

"Yes."

"It was bad enough before, never seeing Toby, never being able to spend any time with you, I mean, *real* time, but I never knew, I never even thought Toby's life could be at stake." The poster on the wall blurred watery. The upper part of her index finger was in her mouth. She was biting on it, hard. "I can't stand this!"

Quietly, Teddy said, "We have to stand this."

"I do love you, Teddy."

Teddy said, "Let's keep doing the best we can." He exhaled. "Are you sleeping?"

"I fell asleep near dawn this morning. I slept a few hours."

"Is Colonel Turnbull there?"

"No." She looked at the end table. The bottle of bourbon had not been touched. "I haven't seen him all day."

"I suggest you find him. Tell him about the car and

the motel. Leave everything in his hands. Try to get some sleep."

"All right, Teddy." She began to hang up, then raised the phone to her ear again. "Teddy?"

"Yes?"

"Sorry about what I said. But we have to do something else."

Teddy said, "It would be nice."

Christina said, "Nothing like this must ever happen to us again."

After she hung up, she turned to get a tissue in the bathroom, not bothering to switch on the bedroom light. She was halfway across the bedroom when a man who had been sitting on the bed stood up.

Thirty-six

"Let me turn on the light," Colonel Turnbull said.

He turned on the bedside lamp.

Christina had one hand on top of the bureau, the other on her breasts. She was trying to suck in breath.

"I'm so sorry to have given you a fright," Colonel Turnbull said. "I was just coming out of the bathroom when I heard you dash in and answer the phone. I didn't want to disturb you." He waved his arm at the tiny bedroom. "There was no place else I could go."

Christina found enough breath to say, "That's all right." She put her foot out toward the bed. "Just let me sit down a moment."

Taking her by the arm, he helped her to sit on the edge of the bed.

He was smiling.

"I'm so sorry," he repeated. "Was that your husband on the phone?"

"Yes." Her pulse was pounding in her ears. "Did you hear everything?"

Again, he waved his arm around the room. "There was nowhere else I could go, you see. Perhaps I should have let you know I was here . . . but you sounded so . . . distraught."

"No," she said. Then she said, "Yes."

"My dear child. Just give yourself a moment to recover. I'm so sorry."

"No, no," she said. "It's all right. I got the registration number of the kidnapper's car. It's right there in my purse."

Colonel Turnbull went into the living room. He picked up the purse from where she had dumped it on the divan. He took out the piece of paper and studied it in the light. Coming back to the bedroom, he put the paper in his pocket.

"Really doesn't help much, I'm afraid," he said. "Not at all, really."

"But Toby was at that motel. Two nights ago. Mr. Silvermine positively identified him!"

"Did he indeed?"

"And he gave me the car registration number. It's a rented car. It hasn't been turned in yet. Can't you find the car?"

"How?"

"The police. Put out an all-points bulletin, or whatever they call it."

"My dear Christina. Don't believe what you hear on television. There are thousands of cars missing in California alone. The police don't find any of them, unless one happens to drop from a helicopter through the police station roof."

"Still—"

"Christina, we are not going to the police on this matter. Do you want this story on the front page of the *San Francisco Examiner, New York Times, London Times* by tomorrow morning? That wouldn't leave your husband much room to negotiate, would it?"

"I don't care!"

"Others do," Colonel Turnbull said primly. "And, too, I'm talking about negotiating for your son's life."

"Your own men! They've been following me for two days. Tell them to go look for the car."

"Yes, of course," he said. "I'll do just that."

He went back into the living room. "You just rest awhile," he said. "I'll be back shortly."

"Why don't you use the telephone here?" she asked.

"I've disturbed you enough," he said at the door. "Get some rest."

Thirty-seven

A young couple scampered past Turnbull on their
way to the tennis courts. The girl's tennis skirt and
panties were so short easily pinchable areas of her
cheeks were showing. The boy's legs were slim and
sinewy.

"Rotten sods," Turnbull muttered.

The boy glanced over his shoulder angrily. The girl
giggled and pulled on the boy's hand.

"It's almost nine," the girl said. "We'll miss the
court."

The double rows of clay courts were superbly
bathed in white light. Most of the players were dressed in whites: shorts, short dresses, jerseys, except for
the odd blue, green or red shirt. All the balls that
went back and forth over the nets were colored—
yellow, pink, red.

To Turnbull, the lit courts were like a station in
space. It was a wholly unreal, synthetic environment,
with intent people hurrying about doing things of
which he had no comprehension.

The tennis courts were for people's pleasure. As
were yacht clubs, ski centers, polo fields, race courses
and other places Teodoro Rinaldi had enjoyed all his
life and understood completely.

Official son: precious little Teodoro.

At the Orphanage of Saints John and Thomas outside Liverpool, where Augustus Turnbull had spent
much of his less than precious youth, only one game
had been encouraged by the staff, a particularly vicious form of rugby. As Turnbull remembered it,
oversized teams of undersized boys would surround a
ball and kick out their aggressions on each other's

bare shins. Every boy was obliged to play. Shinbones
that were not raw and bleeding by the end of the
game drew contemptuous glances from mates and
staff alike.

It was not a game for pleasure. It was a painful tor-
ture, exercised methodically, to keep boys beaten
back and in hand.

He walked along the fence outside the tennis
courts.

"Good shot," he heard someone say.

Turnbull knew what a "good shot" is. A "good shot"
is a shot which gives the victim just enough time to
shit in his pants before dying.

Turnbull had made many "good shots."

The lanky man waiting for Turnbull near Court 7
was watching the people play. Dressed in a gray suit,
hands behind his back, Cord seemed absorbed in the
game.

Turnbull knew Cord was only pretending not to
know Turnbull was behind him.

"Thinking of taking up the game, Simon?" Turnbull
said.

Cord turned slightly to him. "I have played," he
said. "I spent fifteen months in Hong Kong once when
people thought I might be useful there."

"Were you useful there?"

Cord said, "Yes. Had a lot of time off. One of those
stop-and-go situations while the diplomacy boys see-
sawed. Yes," he smiled. "At the end I proved to be
very useful."

"Same employers then as now?"

"No," Cord said. "I have no particular credit with
my current employers."

"You don't deserve much," Turnbull said.

The overhead lights whitened Cord's short gray
hair, long gray face, gray eyes.

"How are things going?" Cord asked.

"Bloody awful!"

"How about giving me some facts, Gus?" Cord asked politely.

"Facts?" Turnbull put his face closer to Cord's and fixed him in the eye. "Fact one: they know we got the boy away from New York by using his own plane reservation. Fact two: they know he's here somewhere in the Bay area. Fact three: they know what motel he stayed at two nights ago. Fact four: they not only have a full and accurate description of this Mullins character, they know his full name and home address." Cord turned his head. "Fact five: they even have the registration number of the car Mullins is using."

Cord's eyes were directed at the tennis players, but they were not focused.

"You're right, Gus. This is bloody awful."

Turnbull hit Cord's shoulder with the heel of his hand.

"One bloody, silly, spoiled bitch has been able to trail you right up to your bloody ass!"

Cord looked at the ground. "The Ambassador's wife? Christina Rinaldi?"

"Rinaldi!" Turnbull shouted.

A tennis player shouted to them, "Quiet, please!" He said to his opponent, "Take two serves."

"Christina Rinaldi," Turnbull finally said.

"Hard to believe." Cord shook his head.

Turnbull took Christina's piece of paper out of his pocket and slammed it against Cord's stomach.

"Hard to believe, eh? This was in Christina's purse. Mullins's name, address, car registration number."

Cord tipped the paper toward the tennis lights to read the handwriting.

"And," Turnbull said, "they know Mullins and the kid are still floating around this area somewhere. Mullins didn't even have the sense to change cars. He's still driving the car he picked up from the airport when he arrived!"

"They said he was thick," Cord said. "Dubrowski's friends said there's nothing between his ears but dead roaches."

Turnbull put his finger against Cord's lapel. "Tell me, Cord, why can't we be perfectly certain right now that Tobias Rinaldi is dead and his body's just waiting for Sunday morning's sunlight to be discovered?"

Cord cleared his throat. "It would be the most natural thing to presume."

"You sound like a ruddy professor!"

"Listen, Turnbull, this is my job—"

"—And a ruddy good job you've made of it, too!"

"Gus, you're out of control. I've got to see this thing through, with or without you. Do you understand?"

Turnbull pushed his finger hard against Cord's chest. "If Mullins has wasted the kid because he doesn't know what else to do, and the kid's body is found tomorrow, you and I have had it. The world isn't big enough for you and me to hide in."

A tennis player was standing inside the fence, peering through the edge of light at them in the shadows. He said quietly, "Are you gentlemen guests here?"

"We own the place," Turnbull said.

"That's not true. Please leave." The tennis player went back to his baseline.

Cord said, "Gus, get control of yourself—or else. Try to keep your sanity—at least until Monday night."

Turnbull hit Cord hard on the side of his head. As Cord staggered off-balance, Turnbull aimed a kick at his groin but instead contacted with his kneecap.

Cord's hands began to rise.

Turnbull hit Cord with all his weight and power just below the short ribs. As Cord fell forward, Turnbull hit him in the face.

A woman screamed.

The tennis player ran back to the inside of the fence.

"Hey!" he yelled.

Cord's head was on the ground. Turnbull kicked it just above the ear.

All the witnesses were on the other side of the tennis fence.

Turnbull turned his back on them and walked out of the lit area. He found a path winding among some rhododendron bushes.

Thirty-eight

"Ah, Colonel Turnbull."

Christina had spent a long time standing under the shower, letting the hot spray play on her neck and shoulders. Dressed in a robe, she had opened her bedroom door to see if Turnbull had returned. Just as she was closing the door, the front door to the bungalow opened and Turnbull stepped in.

"I was looking for you," Christina said. "Thought I'd turn in, see if I have any luck sleeping."

The expression on Turnbull's face Christina had never seen before. His ruddy skin seemed redder than usual. In his eyes, for the first time, seemed to be some recognition of her as a person—a body.

She gathered her robe more lightly around her.

"Before I try to sleep, I just wonder if . . . the car's registration . . ."

Turnbull closed the door behind him. He took a long, narrow black case out of his jacket's inside pocket. He went directly to the tall reading lamp on the divan's end table.

". . . if you'd tell me what I should do next, what we should do next. I'd feel so much better if we had a plan, if I had a plan . . . if I knew what the plan is . . . what . . ."

Turnbull turned around. "You're not supposed to be doing anything, Christina. Just being quiet."

There was a hypodermic syringe in his right hand.

"Let me handle everything from this point."

He held the syringe up to the lamp and pushed the plunger. A colorless fluid jetted from the needle.

"What are you doing?" she asked.

"This won't take a moment." He walked toward her. "Please cooperate."

"No!"

Christina tried to get by him, tried to get to the front door. He grabbed her wrist and swung her around. She felt the back of her leg against the coffee table.

"No!"

Turnbull's left hand was grabbing for her arm.

She pulled it away from him, regained her footing. She put the flat of her hand against his chest and pushed.

Suddenly, Turnbull's left fist smashed against her right cheekbone.

There were darting silver slivers of light against a deep, black field. Her knees were on the floor. She saw the surface of the coffee table.

The flesh of her arm was being squeezed. She pulled in breath. Her cheek was on the coffee table.

She was tumbling, going among, through, the moving silver streaks into the blackness.

Thirty-nine

In Room 39 at the Motel Rancho O'Grady, Spike dropped his newspaper from his bed onto the floor. For a while, he looked at the opposite wall.

Then he said, "Once there was this gang after me—a gang of real badasses—Holy Devils, they called 'em-selves. This was in Passaic, see? Fac' is, I had killed one of their gang members, with a knife. Clean, fair, honest fight, all that. This guy had tromped on my foot at a disco place, see? So I invited him outside, to kill him.

"First, he didn't wanna go, see, 'cause he didn't have no gang with him. But I poked fun at him, and all, and the girls laughed at him.

"So I laughed him into comin' out to get killed.

"He came out with me, back o' this place, and he pulled a knife. I had a knife, too. I only had to sashay around with him a little before I stuck my knife in his eye, see? Deep. . . ."

Spike looked at Toby.

On the other bed, Toby lay on top of his blanket, head on the pillow. Facedown, on his chest was the Uncle Whimsy Comic Book.

Toby was asleep. On his face was a happy smile.

It was ten fifteen. Spike chuckled and turned out the light.

Forty

Christina could not understand what she was doing on the floor. Looking up, she was seeing partly the underside of the coffee table, partly the ceiling.

The telephone was ringing.

Her neck was twisted so that one ear was almost pressing against her shoulder. A part of her face hurt. Her cheekbone. She explored it with her fingers. Her skin stung to the touch.

Sitting up, she discovered her neck was stiff. There was daylight in the room. The reading lamp was still on. She reached up for the telephone. She wanted to stop its ringing.

"Hello?"

"Hello, Mrs. Rinaldi? Christina, it's me. Mary Brown."

"Hello, Mrs. Brown . . . Mary."

"You all right, Christina?"

"I don't know. I guess so."

"You don't sound it."

"Guess I just woke up."

"I know I'm not supposed to be using the Residence's phone long-distance without permission," Mrs. Brown said, "especially for any personal craziness of my own—"

"That's okay."

"I waited until nine thirty. I couldn't figure if it's six thirty in the morning where you are or twelve thirty noon, so I thought I'd be safe if I called at nine thirty. I guess it's six thirty where you are."

It seemed the most natural thing in the world to be chatting with her housekeeper, listening to Mrs. Brown's voice in the morning, dressed in her robe. But why was she sitting on the floor?

"It doesn't cost so much callin' on Sundays, anyway, does it?"

"No. That's all right. I'm glad you called. I suppose I should have called you."

"Well, that's why I'm calling. You're going to think I'm crazy, but I had a dream. And I've been thinking about it. I haven't been sleeping—at all. So last night I took one of those pills Mr. Ambassador keeps in his medicine chest, secondaries or something, you know, sleeping pills?"

"Seconal?"

"Yes. Well, maybe it made me dream. Anyway, it made me sleep. Electronic age. Here's an old woman telling you about her dream over three thousand miles of telephone wire."

"What was it?"

"I dreamt Toby's at Fantazyland."

The fingers of Christina's free hand kneaded the back of her neck.

"Mrs. Rinaldi, you know I'm not someone to believe in dreams. Although, I will say, the Old Testament's full of 'em and I understand some head doctors make a business of 'em. But this dream was too real. I saw Toby. You know Uncle Whimsy's Hat? Fantazyland has made some kind of mountain out of it, and there are rides through it or something. I saw Toby staring up at it. Big bears and rabbits all around him. He was wearing white shorts and a blue shirt. His hand was up, I mean, his arm was, you know? As if his hand was in the hand of someone else—an adult. And then there was this rush of air, and darkness, in my dream, and I felt Toby going through some kind of a tunnel. He was laughing. Crazy, isn't it? But it was so real."

"Mrs. Brown, I'm sure it was real. It was what you wanted to dream. It's what you want to think."

"I thought so, too. I'm not as crazy as all that. Have I ever told you a dream before? I've never had one so real. Then I began thinking. Since three fifteen this morning, when I woke up, after the dream. I've been thinking and remembering certain things."

"Mrs. Brown—"

"Half a moment, Christina. That boy's been determined to get to Fantazyland for longer than you know. More than two years ago, I first heard of it. On the plane, that time we were flyin' to Mexico to talk to them about oil or whatever. I went forward in the cabin to get Toby away to bed and His Majesty had just finished readin' him a chapter of *Winnie-the-Pooh*, and Toby was askin' him, the King, "Will we go to Fantazyland, sir?' and His Majesty looked at the Ambassador, and the Ambassador said, 'Not this trip, Toby. We'll be too far south. Maybe someday we'll get there, if they have us,' and it was I, Mrs. Rinaldi, who took Toby back to the little bunk and strapped him in, and he said he was goin' to Fantazyland. First I'd heard of it. And he's been talkin' about it ever since, to you, to me, to the Ambassador. . . ."

"Yes but—"

"And, by God, Christina, I believe he's there. I know Toby. He's a determined little chap. Knows what he's doing every minute. He looks like he's puttin' up with things, he does, but he's a genius at settin' himself a goal and gettin' there. You don't even see him doin' it. Like his father, he knows how to handle people, and like you, Christina, he knows how to mark time and appear to be patient and then assert himself at just the right moment, in just the right way. Forgive me for complimenting you both. But I know you a great deal better than maybe you think I do, after nine years bein' with you. Great believer in blood, I am, especially where your son, Toby, is concerned. Put Toby on the West Coast of this country, within a few miles of Fantazyland, and, by God, Christina, even bound hand and foot, he'll see himself there."

Christina said nothing: she was envisioning Toby at Fantazyland. Toby had shown her the pictures, too.

Where had the idea of this trip to the West Coast really come from? Christina had thought it was her idea—a family vacation, an attempt to give Teddy a break.

But the timing of it was so bad. Resolution 1176R. Who laid down the timing of this trip?

"Oh, Mrs. Brown. . . ."

"Think I'm crazy if you want. I'll probably think I'm crazy myself after the sun gets a little higher in the sky. Burns away the nighttime fantasies. But I had to tell you about it."

"I'm glad you did."

"A thing like this drives everybody crazy," Mrs. Brown said. "Makes us all do and think crazy things. I'll never take one of those secondaries again. Never had such a real dream."

"I understand. Anything any one of us thinks—"

"Now, what about the carpets?"

"What carpets?"

"I was supposed to get the carpets cleaned while you were gone. No cleaner will take 'em without a billion dollars of insurance."

"Forget about the carpets, Mrs. Brown."

"They do need cleaning. And we've got them up in a big pile in the foyer. Mr. Ambassador's forever trippin' over 'em—"

"Forget about the carpets. I don't give two hoots about the damned carpets. Let 'em rot."

"All right."

"Mrs. Brown . . . Mary. If you think anything else, have any other ideas, call me right away and let me know."

"I tell you what I think, Christina," Mrs. Brown said. "Toby's at Fantazyland."

Forty-one

Over the intercom Sylvia Menninges's voice said, "Mr. Ambassador? Assistant Secretary of State Skinner is here to see you. Says he's just dropped by to say hello."

Ambassador Teodoro Rinaldi's finger hesitated on the intercom button. He glanced at his watch and the typed schedule on his desk. It was twelve thirty-nine, Sunday noon hour. He was due at lunch with the Security Council at one o'clock. It was key he be there, and be there on time. Yesterday, and so far today, he had been keeping his schedule well, continuing, hour by hour, meeting by meeting, word by word, to develop delegate support for Resolution 1176R. He had even managed to meet or talk with most of the people he had missed Friday. He sincerely hoped he had carried it all off well, looking tired, he knew, under pressure, of course. He believed no one had discerned from his performance how distraught, sick at heart, he was.

Now, Pat Skinner, who probably knew the Ambassador's schedule better than the Ambassador himself did, suddenly was dropping in, from Washington, to "say hello"; in fact, to look into the eyes of someone he knew twenty-five years and assess for the diplomatic community Teddy's true condition. Would the Ambassador's appeal to the United Nations the following night be strong, stirring, convincing, successful? Or would it be delivered as one more diplomatic essay, an exaggerated position paper meant to cause nothing more real than slight and slighting reference in subsequent cocktail chatter? The Ambassador knew he could not conceal his true condition from Pat Skinner.

Before he responded, Sylvia Menninges said, "Mr.
Ambassador? Your tailor on 270."

"Your tailor": code for His Majesty. On scrambler.
*Pat Skinner must be standing right next to her desk,
listening.*

Teddy said, "Ask Mr. Skinner to wait a moment,
please. And make sure the car is out front, will you,
please?"

"It's waiting now, sir."

He pushed button 270—the green button. "Sir?"

A long pause, then the funny voice of Donald Duck,
the boss's voice over the scrambler phone.

"Teddy? I'm not hearing any good news."

"Neither am I. Sir."

"How do you feel?"

"All right."

"Do you feel you can carry on?"

"Yes."

"The terrible thing about this, Teddy, is that I don't
see any options. I don't see we have any choice but
for you to carry on. In kidnapping your son, they've
hit you personally. But if you personally don't get up
there in front of the United Nations tomorrow night
and submit Resolution 1176R, it has no chance of
passing. Diplomacy is a personal business. There's no
one I can substitute for you."

"I know that."

"I can't see any plan other than the plan we decided
upon first: that we keep this matter as quiet as possible, and, that you proceed as normally as possible."

"Yes, sir."

"I mean, to the end, Teddy. To the end."

"Yes."

"I have a terrible thing to say."

Teddy waited.

"Teddy, if this Resolution doesn't pass, tanks are
going to roll. They are going to roll across the sands of

this nation, down the streets of our villages, into the cities. It will mean war, Teddy, within the year. The major powers will fight each other on this poor speck of sand. They will destroy this nation over our ability to ship oil through the Persian Gulf. There is no doubt about it. You know this to be true. Don't you, Teddy?"

"Yes. Yes, I do."

"You might be wise to consider that we are at war now. Teddy, your son may be a casualty of that war."

Teddy looked across his office at a complicated tapestry on the far wall.

Teddy said, "He's only eight years old, sir."

"Given a war, Teddy, there will be many eight-year-old casualties."

"I understand."

"I'm asking you to understand and accept something no one can reasonably ask a father of a child to understand and accept. You have to think of your son, no matter how little he is, as a soldier. Right now, they've got him. We cannot permit the utter destruction of this nation and most likely several other nations—if not the world—because of the loss of one soldier."

"I hear you. Sir."

"I think this is the most terrible thing I've ever had to say. No matter what happens, I trust, in time, you'll forgive me. Understand. . . ."

The Donald Duck voice faded off. There was a snap on the line, then a high-pitched whirring noise.

Teddy hung up.

In a moment, the door to his office opened and Pat Skinner stepped around it, his eyes immediately on Teddy's face.

The Ambassador had not signaled Sylvia to permit him to enter. She had seen the yellow light on line 270 go out and knew he was on a tight schedule.

Pat said, "Am I disturbing?"

At first, Pat's look was normally curious. As he came across the office, looking at Teddy, the expression on his face became one of shock and then alarm.

"Ted, are you all right?"

"Haven't been getting all the sleep I should. Burning the candle at both ends."

"That's true, but—" Pat Skinner sat down.

"Figure I'll start a vacation sometime this week. Maybe as early as Tuesday. See how things go Monday night. Maybe I'll even join Christina and Toby out at Fantazyland."

"They're at Fantazyland?"

"Sure. Why not? Toby had a school break. He's been pressing for a trip to Fantazyland for as long as anybody can remember. You know Toby. This seems as good a time as any."

Skinner was now looking as if Teddy had taken leave of his senses.

"Once Toby sets his minds to something . . ." Teddy said.

"I hear you dropped a few stitches Friday."

" 'Dropped a few stitches'?"

"Yeah. Got around the community. Canceled appointments. Not available."

"Oh, that. Had a terrible sore throat. Couldn't speak above a whisper."

"I spoke to you on the phone Friday."

"Right. Then you know what I mean."

"You didn't sound—uh—right."

"Ready to sing Wagner now."

"How do you think things are going? I mean, for the passage of the Resolution? Got your ducks all lined up?"

"It will go down like Kentucky bourbon, Pat. I have no doubt of it. The Resolution is vital not only to our national interests, but essential to the best interests of nearly every nation in the world."

"The Islamic groundswell—"

"—is entirely understandable." Teddy stood up. "I can't be late for lunch, Pat. Not only is it diplomatically essential, but, also, I'm hungry. Can I give you a lift?"

"No. Uh, no. Thanks."

"Let's get together, Pat. I mean, let's get the families together. A weekend somewhere. Chew things over. Maybe after my vacation. . . ."

Forty-two

. . . 7NP 4484 . . . 7NP 4484 . . . 7NP 4484 . . .
7NP 4484 . . . 7NP 4484 . . . 7NP 4484 . . . 7NP
4484 . . . 7NP 4484 . . . 7NP 4484 . . . 7NP 4484
. . . 7NP 4484 . . .
. . . 7NP 4484
7NP 4484!

Dazed as she was, having read thousands of registration plates in Fantazyland's enormous parking lot, driving slowly up and down every row, watching out for children and parents cutting across the lot in front of her every minute (they looking to neither the right nor the left, having been guaranteed every safety while enjoying their stay at Fantazyland), having to argue with at least one parking lot attendant at the end of every row who did not like her driving up and down the rows, insisted she park, ignored her statement that this was an emergency and she was looking for a car and could never walk all those miles, up and down, up and down, driving off on them, driving around them, evading them, ignoring their shouts, mile after mile.

Finally, when she saw it, she stopped. She blinked. Registration number 7NP 4484. A blue two-door car. She read the number again and again. She thought she so much wanted to see it she had created the illusion of seeing it.

No. Right beside her, parked near the front of the Fantazyland parking lot, was a blue car, registration number 7NP 4484.

"Oh, my God. Toby is here!"

Up the row, twenty cars away, was an empty slot.

Christina sped her car into it, locked it and ran back to the blue two-door.

The registration plate still read 7NP 4484.

She peered through the windows to see some evidence of Toby. On the front seat there was an Uncle Whimsy Comic Book. Probably ninety-nine percent of the cars in Fantazyland's parking lot had Uncle Whimsy Comic Books in them. There were some gum wrappers on the floor. Nothing else. The car was as neutral as any other rented car.

She looked around the lot. The men Turnbull had had following her were nowhere in sight. She hadn't seen them all morning. After days of uselessly spooking her, they were not around when she could use them.

Neither were there any parking lot attendants in sight.

In her purse she found a fingernail file. With this, she let the air out of three of the car's tires. Working the release of each tire valve seemed to take forever. She wanted the tires absolutely flat.

It took her as long to work the hood latch. Finally getting it into a position where it had some give to it, she yanked it up, breaking something.

She studied the motor a long moment. She could see nothing obviously devastating to do. There were some black hoses, and she tugged those free. She tugged free every hose and wire she could find, ripping out altogether those that would come.

Finally, she took off her shoe and beat the engine with her heel.

When she was trying to close the hood, she noticed a parking lot attendant had driven up in an electric cart. He had stopped and was looking at the flat tires, the wires on the ground.

"Need help, lady?"

"Somebody vandalized my car!" she said.

"Gosh. . . ."

He stepped off his cart to examine the damage.

Christina said, "I've got to call my husband," and began running across the lot.

"Hey, wait! Lady! I'll give you a lift."

Running across one row, she was nearly hit by a station wagon full of Girl Scouts.

"Stoooo—pid!" yelled all the girls.

UNCLE WHIMSY WELCOMES YOU—ONE AND ALL—TO FANTAZYLAND.

Right at the main gate, to the left of the box offices, was a row of public telephones.

Christina slowed to a walk. She knew the park was enormous. Uncle Whimsy's mountainous Hat was in the middle, and it looked a long way away.

I found the car, I found the car. . . .

Forty-three

When Pat Skinner entered the Waldorf Astoria suite of the United States Ambassador to the United Nations, the Secretary of State was sitting on the divan, shoes off, wriggling his toes. For socks, the Secretary was known to wear only lisle, which, of course, gave rise to jokes about "our Secretary with cold feet." (At the Pentagon, the Secretary of Defense had become referred to, therefore, as "ol' Iron Socks.")

The Secretary of State was due downstairs in a few minutes to give an after-luncheon speech to The National Association of Christians and Jews. The Secretary had arranged to miss lunch. Experience had taught him he was better off sitting alone somewhere, resting, sipping a vodka martini, shoes off, wriggling his toes, than keeping up luncheon and dinner conversations.

"Hallo, Pat!" said the Secretary of State.

Skinner said, "Glad I caught you."

The Secretary jiggled his martini glass and laughed. "Caught me at what?"

At the sideboard Skinner mixed himself a very weak scotch and soda.

"How's your friend Rinaldi? That thing going to work?"

Skinner said, "No. Doubt it. He's a mess."

"How do you mean?"

Skinner sat down. "He looks in such bad shape I don't see how he can make it through the day, let alone tomorrow and tomorrow night."

"Physically?"

"Looks like he should be hospitalized. Mentally, he may have cracked. He had no very reasonable excuse for being incommunicado Friday. Pleaded sore throat, but he had forgotten I had spoken to him on the phone myself. Would you believe his wife and kid are at Fantazyland? You'd think His Majesty would have better use for his illegal secret intelligence in this country these days—I mean, in lining up ducks—than having them escort the Ambassador's wife and child around an amusement park. Teddy is sitting there in his office, being late for lunch with the Security Council while chatting on the phone with his tailor. He's almost incoherent. All he talked to me about was his vacation and that he's ready to sing Wagner."

"Wagner?"

"Wagner."

The Secretary of State said, "Nobody's ever ready to sing Wagner." He stared into the dark fireplace. "Some guys just can't take the pressure. I'll inform the President. I'm stopping to pick him up at Camp David at five o'clock. Want a ride in the chopper?"

"I think I'd better stay here. What will the President say?"

The Secretary shrugged. " 'Pull.' He'll say, 'Pull.' " He drained his glass. "The old boy's in no mood to back another dead horse. This administration has already bought so many we can supply a glue factory for a decade."

The Secretary put his glass down and leaned over to tie on his shoes. "Surprising. Thought Teddy had more stuff in him. We all react to pressure in this business, Skinner. Trick is to let no one see it." Red-faced, the Secretary sat up. "Not even," he said, "your alleged best friend."

Forty-four

"Sylvia? Quick! This is Christina Rinaldi. Get me the Ambassador!"

Phone to one ear, fingers pressed against the other, Christina ran her eyes along the lines of people waiting for tickets at Fantazyland's box offices.

"I'm sorry, Mrs. Rinaldi. The Ambassador is at a special luncheon meeting with the United Nations Security Council."

"Can you transfer me somehow?"

"No. I'm sorry, I can't."

"It's terribly important."

"Mrs. Rinaldi, even the President of the United States isn't allowed to interrupt a special meeting of the Security Council."

"Oh, dear."

"Christina, can't I take a message?"

"Yes. Get to Teddy as soon as you can."

"I will."

"Tell him I found the car. He'll know what I mean. In the parking lot at Fantazyland."

"You found the car."

"The car we were looking for. Willins'-Doland's-Jackson's-Mullins's car."

"Wait, I didn't get all those names."

"Never mind. He'll know which car I mean. Tell him I'm at Fantazyland now, and I need help. I need a lot of help. Tell him to tell Major Mustafa I need people here now."

"You need people at Fantazyland."

"And, Sylvia. Tell him not to trust Colonel Turnbull."

"Not to trust Colonel who?"

"Turnbull. You don't know him. Last night he stuck a needle in my arm. Gave me some kind of drug—a sedative. Do you have that?"

"Yes. I think so."

"Get to Teddy as fast as you can, tell him these two things and ask him to get people here as fast as he can."

"To Fantazyland?"

"Yes. To Fantazyland."

Forty-five

"Look at them flowers!" Spike said. He and Toby were in the garden of Princess Daphne's Flower Palace. "I knever knew there was so many different kinds'a roses."

"What roses?" Toby said.

"Those roses."

"Those are tulips," Toby said.

"Yeah, tha's right, kid. They're tulip roses."

"No," Toby said. "Those are daffodils."

"Did I ast you? Punk kid. Whaddayou know? I said those are daffadil-kind of tulip roses."

Toby pointed. "Those are roses over there. On the trellis."

"Talkin' fancy again, uh? Thought I knocked that outa you."

"What's fancy in what I said?"

"These flowers out here are nicer than them inside Princess Daphne's pad," Spike said. "These are real, you see, real flowers growing in the earth."

Toby said, "I think they're fresh planted."

"Don't be wise, punk. The ones inside were phonies. Dincha know that? They was glass and plastic and stuff like that."

A barefoot girl dressed entirely in flowers drifted by them. Flowers were twisted neatly in her hair. She carried a yellow sunflower.

Watching her, Spike said, "I'd like to pluck her."

"Shh," Toby said. "That's Princess Daphne."

The girl looked at Spike. Her face reddened. Either she was blushing or angry.

"Aw," Spike said, "she's nothin' more than a Uncle Whimsy groupie gettin' the minimum wage."

"Come on over here, Spike," Toby said. "There are some more roses."

"Yeah!" Spike said. "I never seen a garden like this!"

*

Spike wanted to drive a bumper car again, so he did. He smashed into everyone he could with maximum force, calling everybody in sight "Bastid!," shaking his fist in all directions at once, not seeing any cars that came at him from his left.

Toby watched through the fence. He had had his last bumper car ride with Spike.

Toby did get him to go with him through The Hall of Knives.

In the first room they came to, there was a polite, museumlike display of every sort of knife, sword, dagger ever invented by man. In the next room, some people in baggy trousers performed a sword dance. In the third room, furnished as a banquet hall, two cavaliers fought a duel down stone steps, across the room, up onto and along the dining table, scattering roast pigs and fowls and wine glasses.

Then they were walked through a dark, scary, menacing place. Knives flew through the air. A guillotine clanged down just as they passed it. A great, gleaming, sharpened pendulum swung over their heads, dropping lower and lower. A huge barrel, spinning seemingly out of control, rolling on armatures, approached them from the dark. Swords stuck out all sides of it, at all angles.

The tourists smiled and laughed and applauded and took pictures.

Spike backed into the far railing. His face was ashen.

*

Then they went back to Wild West City to try the shooting gallery again.

Forty-six

Sylvia Menninges followed the Ambassador into his office.

"The luncheon ran late," he said.

He sat at his desk.

Sylvia said, "Mrs. Rinaldi called."

"Oh?"

"She left a message. She was talking so fast I had trouble getting it all down." Sylvia looked at her steno pad. "First she said she found the car and that you would know what that means."

"She did? She found the car?"

Sylvia nodded. "In the parking lot at Fantazyland."

Teddy sat back. "Well, I'll be damned."

Sylvia read from her pad. "Please ask Major Mustafa to send people, a lot of people, to assist her right away."

"Major Mustafa?" Teddy wrinkled his brow. "Why Major Mustafa?"

"I don't know. She also said you were not to trust a Colonel Turnbull."

"She said that?" Teddy looked extremely curious. "Why did she say that?"

"She said . . . Colonel Turnbull, I guess she meant . . . gave her a sedative last night."

"I see." Teddy's face returned to normal. "I see. I'm sure Christina needed a sedative. I'm also sure she resented the hell out of being slipped one. Okay." He sat up and looked at the papers Sylvia had put on his desk since he had left. "Get on to Colonel Turnbull immediately. Tell him Christina has found the car we've been looking for in the parking lot of Fantazy-

land and he and his men are to join her there immediately."

"Shall I say anything to Major Mustafa?"

"No," Teddy said. "Leave everything in the hands
of Colonel Turnbull."

Forty-seven

Cord had followed Christina from the bungalow.

He had parked where he was directed to park in Fantazyland's huge lot and then stood by his car, looking over the rooftops of other cars sparkling in the sunlight. He watched her drive up and down the rows of parked cars, evading the attendants who yelled and waved at her. He figured she was looking for Mullins car, but he had no idea what led her to look for the car in Fantazyland's parking lot.

He saw her stop near the front of the lot, in front of a blue two-door car. She parked nearby. Watching her, he began walking at an angle among the cars to where she was. She ran from her car back to the blue two-door.

From a distance, he watched her flatten the car's tires, break open the hood and rip things out of the engine.

When the attendant in the electric cart came along, she ran toward the main entrance to Fantazyland.

By the time Cord got there, she was using one of the telephones.

He waited in one of the box office lines. After telephoning, she got into his line, about a dozen people behind him. Simon Cord preceded Christina Rinaldi into Fantazyland.

When she came through the main gate, he was standing, hands behind his back, listening to the music from the bandstand.

*

Cord ambled into the shade of a giant pink mushroom and stopped. A child went by, accidentally brushing his cotton candy against the sleeve of Cord's gray suit. He brushed it off and looked at his watch. It was five minutes past five.

Christina Rinaldi, dressed in a light, beige suit, was standing near the cotton candy stand. Her eyes were roaming high and low in each direction, methodically. She was alone.

Slowly, she began to move in the sunlight in the direction pointed by a sign saying, TO THE PAST.

At a good distance to the side and a little behind her, keeping in the shade as much as possible, at her pace, Cord followed her.

She was passing a carousel, slowly, looking at the children revolving on it, the air filled with the loud, clanging carousel music, *London Bridge is falling down.* . . . After watching it go around once, she looked off to her left.

Suddenly, Christina's body braced as if jolted by an electric shock. She was screaming. She was yelling something.

She began to run.

Cord glanced down the slope to see what she was seeing, but saw only a crowd of tourists going through the fortlike gates of Wild West City.

A man ran past her. In his left hand was a gun. He reached the crowd at the gate wall before her and began to weave through them, pushing and shoving, waving his gun.

The people smiled and stepped aside for him.

Another man ran up behind Christina, a man wearing an Uncle Whimsy T-shirt under his jacket. As he passed her, he pushed Christina's shoulder, making her land too hard on her right shoe heel, snapping it. As she fell to the walkway's hard surface, he spilled his bag of peppermints. By the time he got to the crowded Wild West City gate, he, too, had a gun in his hand.

The people smiled and let him through.

Smiling, they even let long-legged Cord stride through.

In the middle of the main street of Wild West City, a cowboy, wearing a black hat, black shirt, black patch over one eye, was cracking a bullwhip and snarling.

Among the whipcracks was a gunshot. The cowboy's head jerked toward the gate. He saw two men running toward him with drawn guns. The cowboy dropped his whip, vaulted a water trough and dropped to the ground, facedown, hands over his hat.

Down the street, Cord saw a man and a boy. They looked around.

Toby Rinaldi and . . . Mullins.

There was another pistol shot.

Three constables came out of the crowd at the entrance gate and began running down the street.

The marshall came out of his office. He looked for the whip-cracking villain. There was another gunshot and the marshall ducked back into the office.

Mullins and Toby ran to their right, up onto a raised-board sidewalk.

The two men fired at them nearly simultaneously.

At the end of the block, Mullins tripped off the sidewalk. He stumbled in the street. The child ran back for him, grabbed his arm and pulled him along.

None of the tourists screamed or backed away.

The tourists smiled and laughed and applauded and took pictures.

Mullins and the boy were halfway up the next block. The man in the Uncle Whimsy T-shirt fired again into the crowd.

Cord could see neither the boy nor Mullins.

The crowd did not disperse. They laughed at the two men, standing in the middle of the street, their faces agape.

The three constables, mustaches bobbing, billy clubs in hand, were running up the street toward them. The helmet of one fell off. Long, blond hair streamed behind her.

The men stuffed their guns into their pockets and took off at an angle to each other. One ran through the swinging doors of a saloon. The other went up the street before darting through the open door of The Glassware and China Shoppe. The constables ran after them.

The tourists gave a hearty round of applause.

*

Down the street, Christina was standing by the gate, her shoes in her hand. Even from a block away, Cord could see her eyes moving wildly.

She had a black eye.

Moving at an angle, Cord walked half a block to where he had last seen Mullins and the boy.

It was not obvious from a distance, but there was a narrow space between two frame buildings, covered by a board fence. Cord pushed against it with his fingers. It swung open. He stepped through it.

There was a narrow alley running between the two buildings. At the far end of the alley were covered garbage buckets.

Cord walked to them and turned the corner of the building. Near the back wall were scuff marks in the dirt. He crouched.

In the dirt was half-dried blood.

Cord stood up and looked around. It was becoming dusk. The light in the alley was diminishing rapidly.

He went back and forth, up and down, but could find no more blood. He could not discover which way Mullins and the boy had gone.

He went back down the alley and through the fence. There was almost no one in the main street.

But in the middle of it, shoes in hand, the shoulder of her suit jacket torn, staring at him as he came through the gate, was Christina Rinaldi.

UNCLE WHIMSY IS GLAD YOU HAVE ENJOYED YOUR DAY AT FANTAZYLAND BUT NOW MUST BID YOU GOOD NIGHT SO ALL UNCLE WHIMSY'S FRIENDS CAN GET THEIR REST AND COME OUT TO PLAY TOMORROW.

A woman's voice sang over the loudspeakers: *Good night until tomorrow . . . Sweet dreams you shall have . . .*

Cord turned left and walked along with his head down until Christina was no longer watching him.

Forty-eight

Had there been, or had there not been, a shooting incident at Fantazyland that afternoon?

The question was bursting Drew Keosian's gut.

He stood at the podium, waiting for the last few constables to straggle in after patrolling the grounds one last time before complete dark. They were to make sure all the guests of Fantazyland had returned to their homes, hotels, motels, campers to dream their sweet dreams so they could come out to play tomorrow.

Infrequently, but occasionally, they would discover someone still on the grounds, incredibly drunk (only beer was provided at Fantazyland) or stoned, after closing. Once they found an old senile woman wandering; another time, a veteran lying in a path, immobilized because the metal pin in his hip had suddenly disintegrated. Another time the body of a thirteen-year-old girl had been found, abandoned by her terrified friends when she had died of a coronary infarction in the Doll Museum.

More frequently, they had to search for the missing child while keeping frantic parents calm in Drew's office. Almost invariably, the child was found asleep somewhere, under a bush or near the waterfall. (They had learned from experience to look first for sleeping children near the waterfall.)

There were always the two or three cars left in the parking lot without explanation. Had friends met or been made and gone off in one car? Had engine trouble or personal illness gone unreported but just caused the car to be left there overnight? The next day they would be gone. There were seldom the same cars there for more than one night. About six stolen cars a year were found abandoned in Fantazyland's parking lot.

Through the window Drew could see the headlights of the electric patrol tricycles still pulling up.

At thirty-seven, Drew Keosian was a professional lawman of a rare type. A graduate of Oral Roberts University, he had had his early police training with the Chattanooga, Tennessee, police force. He hated having to deal with the poor, the disenfranchised, the ill, the violent.

Drew believed absolutely in the thick line between the lawful and the lawless, right and wrong, good and evil. He loved his job at Fantazyland. He considered it a great moral experiment, an imitation of God's creating Eden. Fantazyland was a beautiful garden filled with innocence, where people could be children forever. It was his job to make this moral experiment work.

As Chief constable he had few, if any, of the problems of chiefs of police forces of similar size. In his eight years at Fantazyland there had been only one serious crime, and that was the rape of an employee, an older lady who worked at a hot dog stand. There was the occasional purse mislaid. Every few months a gang of pickpockets would work Fantazyland for a day, but the constables were trained to spot them quickly and deal with them summarily. There was some petty shoplifting.

Fantazyland was private property. Constables could and would deny obviously drunk, stoned, or seemingly disturbed people entrance. Everyone coming into Fantazyland was scrutinized by at least one constable.

It was Drew's job to keep the snake from Eden, to keep genuine evil from Fantazyland, and he took it as his holy mission to do so.

An hour or two earlier, Constable Hidgson had phoned in breathlessly saying there were two men firing guns in the middle of Wild West City. Tourists. Real guns.

Drew had hurried to Wild West City (he had not run; the tourists might be alarmed) and found nothing in particular going on.

The cowboy villain told him people were shooting at him, and he didn't like it. The cowboy marshall said he wasn't sure. He said he had come out onto the boardwalk, not seen the cowboy villain, saw the whip on the ground, yet heard what he thought were whip-cracks. He wasn't absolutely sure what else he had seen.

Constable Gladstein told him there had been no shooting as far as he knew, but he might have been on his break at that moment.

Before him now in the police station briefing room, all the constables were seated in their chairs, all with their helmets off, some with their mustaches off, the black handlebar mustaches of the rest clashing weirdly with their blond, brown, red or even natural black hair.

From the podium, Drew asked, "Any bodies tonight? Anyone missing, drunk, lost?"

There was no response.

He said, "Box office tells us supposedly there's an eight-count difference between ins and outs. Eight people who entered Fantazyland today but didn't leave it." He looked at the roomful of tired constables. "Anybody seen any strays? No?"

The chief parking lot attendant (the only person in the room dressed in khaki; the night watchmen wore undecorated blue suits) said, "Drew? There are seven automobiles left in the parking lot tonight."

"Seven? That's unusually high."

"One looks like it's been vandalized. Three flat tires. Motor wires and hoses on the ground."

"No one complained?"

"Yes and no. Jack Dibbs said the lady who owned or rented the car spoke to him and ran off saying she was going to call her husband. He must have come and picked her up."

"I see. Anything else unusual?" Drew Keosian felt his stomach muscles tighten. "Hidgson, what about this shooting incident you reported?"

"Three of us saw it," he said.

Katy chimed in right away. "Two men with handguns ran into Wild West City and fired several shots. Couldn't tell what they were firing at."

Katy, at twenty-three, was the most definite member of the force. Her reports were always the most clear, succinct and certain. Two months before, she had identified and turned in Alf Worsham, known pickpocket. His own pockets were clean, but the state of California was grateful to collect Worsham, anyway, as there were several bad check charges outstanding against him.

"Was it some kind of a gag?" Drew asked.

Katy said, "I don't think so."

"Who was the third constable?"

"I was," Mac Innes said.

"Do you think it was a gag?"

"Guess so. Musta been blanks. Couldn't been shootin' like that, really shootin', without hittin' somebody."

"Did you apprehend these characters?"

"Got away," Hidgson said. "We waited in turns at the main gate, but couldn't recognize them as they went out—if they went out the main gate."

"Description?"

"Two men," Katy said. "One wore an Uncle Whimsy T-shirt."

"No one has complained," Drew said carefully. "That right?"

The constables looked at each other and at him.

Drew exhaled slowly. "Must have been a gag. Remember that time that gang from some fraternity got naked out at the ice cream parlor and sang, *Beat me, daddy, eight to the bar* . . . ? You weren't here then, Katy."

"We caught them," Mac Innes said.

"We could pick them out of the crowd," Hidgson said.

Drew said, "Okay, everybody. See you tomorrow."

Drew went into his office. His hands were shaking. *Katy did not think it was a gag.*

If there had been a shooting incident at Fantazyland this afternoon—even as a gag—the public must never, never know about it.

Forty-nine

"Shit, Toby. They took down ol' Spike."

"Shh."

"They got me. They shot me. They put a bullet in me."

Spike was lying on the floor of Ms. Lillyperson's Cottage, clutching the calf of his leg. His hand was covered with blood.

Toby was sitting cross-legged near him. He was peering through the cottage's second-story dormer window.

Outside, Ms. Lillyperson's residence looked a gray-stone cottage on a rise above the walkway up to Princess Daphne's Flower Palace. Inside, it looked like a packing crate.

"Not in you," Toby said. "They put a bullet through you. Through your leg."

Toby already had rolled up Spike's pant leg and examined the wound. He thought it something, seeing Spike's zebra sock all bloody.

"Never thought nobody would get ol' Spike down. Who'd want to shoot me?"

"Somebody. . . ." Toby said.

"Yeah, kid. Somebody shot me. Who?"

"Fac' is . . ." Toby said, "I dunno."

"Shootin' ol' Spike. I didn't think it was real. Never saw those guys before in my life."

"Shh," Toby said. "Be quiet."

Through the window, Toby watched an electric patrol tricycle go up the path. Its headlight was on. The man driving it was not wearing a constable's uniform, just blue pants and shirt. It went over the hill.

"When it's really dark, I'll bring you over to that log

cabin," Toby said. "The burning log cabin. On the island. Nobody will find us there. Come on. Let me make a tourniquet for your leg."

"Yeah? A tourniquet? You know about things like that?"

"Sure," Toby said. "I got to find the stuff first. A stick and a hunk of rope, or cloth."

"Yeah?"

"I'll be right back."

"Sure," Spike said. "Sure. Only, just don't get lost, kid."

Fifty

Once inside Wild West City, Christina had not understood what was happening. Through the milling crowd on the main street she had seen three constables chasing the two men with guns. About a block and a half up a street, she saw the two men stop, face the buildings to the right, then turn and run in different directions.

Carrying her shoes, the shoulder of her suit torn, Christina then wandered up and down the main street of Wild West City, as she had spent a day wandering in the airport, looking for she knew not what—some sign of Toby, some clue. She was only dimly aware of the fading light, dimly aware of the thinning crowd looking at her: a disheveled, distraught woman, prowling aimlessly, staring intently.

The street was nearly empty. She heard the announcement Fantazyland was closing for the night.

A man came through the board fence in the middle of the block. His pale eyes looked at her expressionlessly. He turned to his left, walked up the boardwalk and around the corner.

Leaving Wild West City, Christina went to her right. Small safety lights, inset in the path, came on. She went off the path to her left, down to a small gulley where there were bushes, and took off her torn pantyhose. She rolled them in a ball and, putting her broken pair of shoes with them, stuffed them under a bush. The ground felt cool and soothing on the stinging soles of her bare feet. She remembered the pleasant sensation from being a kid on her Uncle Toby's farm, summertimes in Pennsylvania.

A constable on an electric patrol tricycle trundled by her. Watching him from the bushes, Christina restrained herself from calling out, explaining everything, asking for help. Fantazyland was enormous. It was becoming dark. Toby was here somewhere. And his kidnapper now knew he was being pursued. Making its little noise, the cart disappeared around a curve to the right.

Stumbling on bruised feet, her ankles becoming increasingly scratched, Christina spent hours wandering around Fantazyland in the dark.

Softly: "Toby . . . ?"

". . . Toby?"

"Toby . . ."

Occasionally, at a distance, she would see the headlight of an electric patrol vehicle jiggling along a path.

More than once, in the dark, she would realize she had returned to an area she thought she had left far behind her. The paths went in deceptive circles. A small moon rose. She stayed away from the turn-of-the-century square just inside the main gate. She knew some administration offices were there, including the police station. The hard, white, metallic, glossy surfaces of The City of The Future aggravated her: there seemed to be no nooks or crannies, no places to peer into, no places for people to hide. The area around Uncle Whimsy's mountainous Hat was completely fenced off and locked. She wandered again through Wild West City, trying every door, through every building that was unlocked, found the alleys, prowled them.

"Toby . . . ?"

And Pirate's Cove, and the Pirate's Caravelle, and The Victorian Graveyard (a few hands sticking above the graves, pasty in the moonlight), and Princess Daphne's Flower Garden.

In The Mercantile Establishment (Notions, Novelties & Sundries) she heard something clatter to the floor behind her.

"Toby!"

No answer.

". . . Toby?"

Again, standing deep in The Pirate's Cove, she thought—she was certain—she heard someone breathing.

"Toby . . ."

The sound stopped.

She found herself, exhausted, in topographically the lowest area of Fantazyland, The Swamp. She stood for a moment at its edge, her sore bare feet enjoying the dampness of the earth.

Behind her, to her right, was the white Riverboat at its dock. Beyond that, the bare spars and crow's nest of The Pirate's Caravelle rose against the sky. Ahead of her, what little moonlight there was reflecting on the river's surface made stark the jungle tree trunks and branches.

She walked, the mud becoming deeper, into the trees along the riverbank.

At one point, stopped, listening, she heard a twig snap.

"Toby!"

There was no answer.

The mud was up to her ankles. She went up the bank, looking for drier ground.

She walked into a tangle of foul-smelling fur.

She jumped back.

Above her was the massive head of a bear. Its eyes glittered in the moonlight. The head was moving. Its upright arm descended toward her.

Christina's hand grabbed her mouth. She screamed.

A mechanical voice said, "Grr."

Christina stumbled backward. Her hair snagged in the branches of a tree.

She turned and scrambled up the slope.

Fifty-one

Billy Joe Carfer stopped the patrol vehicle at the top
of the rise overlooking, to his right, the river, The Riverboat, The Pirate's Caravelle—beyond that, the lake.
To his left were the roofs and fake stone turrets of
Princess Daphne's Flower Palace. Well behind him,
but still looming like a black hole in the sky, was Uncle Whimsy's goony great Hat.

He performed his midnight ritual.

Other night watchmen had a break for coffee or a
sandwich and soft drink. Billy Joe believed coffee
made him nervous. He was seldom hungry. He had
been told enough times soft drinks were bad for his
teeth.

Settling back in his seat, putting one work boot up
against his handlebar, he took a cigarette box out of
his shirt pocket. He did not smoke cigarettes, either.
Cigarettes caused cancer.

Billy Joe unwrapped his joint from its tinfoil, lit up
and inhaled deeply. Pot caused pleasant sensations.

Billy Joe had no feelings about his job as a Fantazyland night watchman. Fantazyland was weird. Per-
verted. Fantazyland's message to the world was: rats
are cute, lions are cowardly, ducks make puns; pirates
are heroes, astronauts are Boy Scouts, outlaws are
comic. From all the signs around Fantazyland one had
to think the only threatening things in all this world
were paying customers. Don't touch this. Don't touch
that. His boss, Drew Keosian, was a turkey. He talked
about Fantazyland as if it were the United States
Constitution, to be protected from overt and covert ag-
gression from all sources and at any cost.

Fantazyland offered a world view—something in

· which to believe. It was a religion. A fenced-in religion.

Billy Joe did not consider his job as work. Nothing ever happened. Being a night watchman at Fantazyland was like being a scarecrow in a cactus patch.

The job permitted him to spend his days painting. Or so he had planned.

His goal was thirty great canvasses. Including the few good works he had kept upon graduating from U.C.L.A., he now felt he had twelve good canvasses.

He had never sold any, but he felt—he just knew— that if he put thirty good canvasses together, any broker, agent, gallery owner, critic would be able to perceive the certainty of his style, the consistent high level of his ability.

Trouble was, he hadn't painted anything in over three months. California days were full of distractions: swimming pools, beaches, movies, girls, galleries filled with other people's work. . . .

As he inhaled his midnight joint, the view of Fantazyland laid out before him took on a delightful aspect. He only smoked grass while on the grounds of Fantazyland. The irony pleased his sensibilities. The lights along the paths became softer. The amusement park objects, ships and castle turrets and the enormous Hat, took on an incredible, stark, funny reality. The fantasy became abstract. One could believe anything, believe one was seeing anything. Polonius pot.

Tonight Billy Joe Carfer heard a woman scream. One loud, protracted, frightened scream. He heard it come from the riverbank, down to his right.

Billy Joe chuckled.

He knew, intellectually, he really had not heard a woman scream.

If nothing else, the study of art had taught Billy Joe Carfer that any perception can be distorted. Reality is better perceived slightly distorted.

After his pot break, Billy Joe Carfer started his electric patrol wagon and joggled down the path to scoot around Princess Daphne's Flower Palace, pass The Hall of Knives, Spooky House. . . .

After his midnight joint, Billy Joe Carfer got a real thrill out of cornering his patrol vehicle at speeds up to twelve miles per hour.

Fifty-two

Goddamn everybody.

Colonel Augustus Turnbull gave his suit coat, bunched under his head, a punch with his fist.

He was lying on the bench along the inside wall of Fantazyland's Victorian Station. The bench was made of horizontal rolls of wood. It dipped considerably before joining its back. Lying on his back or front was impossible. Lying on his side, facing forward, Colonel Turnbull was too fat to fit his hips securely into the dip. His belly hung over the edge of the bench, pulled him toward the floor.

His three men were sprawled around the railroad station. One, on the floor, was snoring loudly.

"Stop that snoring!" Turnbull roared.

The snoring did not stop.

Augustus Turnbull recalled an incident that had happened almost twenty years before, when he had come back from his years as a mercenary in Africa and rejoined the British Army.

He had gone to London for a night on the town. He was a noncommissioned officer, nearly thirty years old. He wore his uniform because that was all he had to wear. For two or three hours he had done whiskey-beer at a pub off Fleet Street. His uniform was sweaty and crumpled. Cigarette ashes had spilled on it.

Finally, there had been a girl to talk to. He bought her drinks and told her stories of the people he had killed. War stories, when there had been no wars she had heard of.

She said, "Be a good laddie and get us a cab. We'll go to my place."

He looked at his drink. "Now?"

"Before it's too late for you, sweets," she said.

So they stumbled out into the street, his arm around her shoulder. Taxi drivers ignored them.

"Come on," she said. "We can get one up at that posh hotel up there."

There were no taxis outside the hotel.

There was a Rolls-Royce saloon car waiting. The uniformed chauffeur standing by the car's back door did not even look at the soldier and the girl swaying on the sidewalk.

He opened the back door.

Three young women in evening gowns and furs and jewels, chatting and laughing, skipped out of the hotel and into the back seat. Two young men in black tie accompanied them. They, too, climbed into the back seat.

"Oooo," the girl with Turnbull said. "Look at them. The pashas."

The chauffeur did not close the car door. He waited. They all waited.

One of the young men finally shouted through the back door at the hotel entrance.

"Rinaldi! Come on!"

Turnbull turned.

A slim, attractive man in his early twenties, beautifully groomed, wearing black tie, ran out of the hotel. The young people in the car cheered as he jumped into the back seat, laughing. He sat among the beautiful women, the jewels, the furs.

The chauffeur closed the door carefully, softly, then ran around to the driver's seat. Even the car's exhaust seemed an expensive perfume.

As it drove off, Turnbull watched through the rear window the heads of gilded youth, chatting, laughing.

It was the first time he had seen Teodoro Rinaldi. *Precious Teodoro.*

An hour later, the girl threw Turnbull out of bed.

Now, in The Victorian Railroad Station at Fantazyland, he gave the tweed suit coat bunched under his head another punch.

"Goddamn," he said softly.

Fifty-three

Exhausted, Christina sat by the waterfall awhile. So many nights as a young girl in Pennsylvania, she had sat out, enjoying the night, dreaming of a husband, children. *Children. . . . Child. . . . Toby. . . .*

Now, even though she leaned against nothing, tried to keep her back straight, her breathing became deeper, more rhythmical. Her chin rested on her collarbone.

She snapped her head awake and watched the headlight of a patrol vehicle as it came along a path, closer to her. It veered off to her left.

It approached a dim square of light in the hillside.

It disappeared.

It took her a long moment to realize the vehicle had gone into the patch of light. Actually gone into it.

It had gone into a tunnel.

She got up and walked toward the patch of light. She was at the rear of Fantazyland, next to The Victorian Graveyard. In the dark, she went through a garden of plastic flowers. They cut the insteps of her feet badly.

There was a chain-linked fence outside the tunnel. The sign was red, with black lettering. DANGER! EMPLOYEES ONLY—SERVICE AREA.

The gate was open. She went through it and a few meters along the path entered the tunnel.

She heard the hum of machinery.

Inset into the base of the tunnel's walls, spaced widely, were lights covered with frosted glass.

The tunnel was cement floored, walled and roofed, of good dimensions, about four meters high. It was wide enough for two patrol vehicles to pass each other. Ahead twenty meters the tunnel curved, dipped smoothly to the left, went back, deeper, under the ground level of Fantazyland.

Half awake but fascinated, Christina padded along. After she passed the curve, the tunnel flattened out.

She passed double steel doors to her left. DANGER! HIGH VOLTAGE AREA. GREEN CARD EMPLOYEES ONLY. There were more such doors to her right. She heard voices. A radio playing. Light spilled into the tunnel from her right. On tiptoes she approached the door and peeked through its small, round window.

A bake shop. She could smell the bread and pastry. There were bakers baking. One, whose elbow had been dipped in flour, was saying, ". . . massage parlors that don't do nothin' for you are a crock a shit. I mean, they know you can't complain to no Chamber of Commerce or . . ."

She crossed the tunnel to the far wall and continued. Shortly, the tunnel widened. There were sidewalks on both sides. Christina began passing many closed doors. They were the sort you'd see in any office building. Stenciled on them were signs which read, CREDIT UNION, Ms. Jameson; HEALTH; COSTUMES, Mr. Roark.

Elevators were between some of the office doors. They were marked: Area 12, BLUE MUSHROOM; Area 9 OUTHOUSE; Area 9, SALOON KITCHEN. Wide corridors went off to the right and left. Yellow lights blinked at the intersections. There were sidewalks and doors in these corridors as well. In the roof of the tunnel, behind grilles, air conditioners whirred.

More doors: Maintenance SPEED TUNNEL Red Card Employees; Maintenance HALL OF KNIVES Red Card Employees; Maintenance SPOOKY HOUSE LIFTS Red Card Employees. . . .

She went by two lit locker rooms. From one she could hear a shower running and a man singing *Blue Moon*.

From across the corridor, Christina looked into a small, lit lounge area. A man in blue shirt and slacks sat doubled over in a chair, changing his boot laces. He did not look up as she glided by.

A ramp swooped down on her right. REPAIR VEHICLES ONLY.

More doors: POST OFFICE; SECRETARIAL, Mr. Tanney; ACCOUNTING, Ms. Engel.

Christina came to a large, semidark room. Its entrance was wide and doorless.

Peering into it, her eyes adjusted. It was a large lounge, comfortable chairs, divans, big tables with lamps and magazines neatly on them. There was a television against each of the three walls. Crepe paper streamers dangled from the walls. A homemade sign read: SO LONG, MARTY! Another read: MAINTENANCE DEPT. WILL MISS YOU, MARTY! There were paper cups on some of the tables, and depleted hors d'oeuvre trays.

In the light from the corridor, Christina found a hunk of cheese on one tray. She sat on a divan in the back of the room and dry-swallowed the cheese.

Her feet were stinging.

Am I just going on instinct? Why can't I figure out where Toby is rationally . . . ?

Sitting on the divan in the back of the semidark lounge, feeling her feet sting, Christina realized that if she had not been having a drug reaction from Turnbull's shot, she probably would not have reacted to Mrs. Brown's dream and looked for the car at Fantazyland. In the condition she was in when Mrs. Brown called, sitting on the floor in her robe, her cheekbone throbbing, her neck aching, her arm sore, her housekeeper's voice over the phone appeared to Christina to have the certainty of God. Toby is at Fantazyland. Christina was off the floor, dressed, and had her foot jammed on the accelerator, headed for Fantazyland, before she knew what she was doing.

Of course, she had had nothing else to do. She had spent all Friday wandering around the airport for no rational reason.

At least she had caught a glimpse of Toby. And he was dressed in white shorts and a blue jersey. . . .

Christina curled up on the divan. But, she told herself, for only a moment, a short moment. . . .

&

Something awoke her. Some noise. She glanced toward the dim light from the corridor. Again, Christina was certain she heard breathing. Someone sniffed.

Quietly, she got up and padded across the room.

Between the divan and the door was a tall-backed Naugahyde chair. Asleep in it was the man she had seen before. The gray-eyed man who had come through the fence in Wild West City and looked at her.

Quietly, breathing through her mouth, she looked at him closely.

He was gray haired; his face was long and sallow; his suit was gray. Some blood vessels had been broken recently on his nose and upper lip. There was a large bump above one ear. Beneath his short hair, on the bump, there was a hairline, half-moon cut. His hands were folded in his lap, his fingers lightly laced.

Softly Christina tiptoed out of the lounge.

She went to the left along the corridor, having no idea in this underground world what time it was.

Fifty-four

"Jeez. This is the coldest house afire I ever been in."

Spike was lying on his back on the floor of The Burning House. He was soaking wet and shivering violently. The raging flames were turned off for the night, but everywhere there was the slightly oniony smell of gas.

After full darkness, they had crawled out of Ms. Lillyperson's Cottage and worked their way down to the swamp and along the riverbank until they were just across from The Burning House Island. Looking across, they could even see in the moonlight the silhouettes of the Indian mannequins attacking the house.

"How deep is the river?" Spike asked. "You go first."

"Not deep, I guess."

"I've lost a whole lotta blood."

"The river will wash out your cut."

" 'Cut!' Some cut. Some dude shot me!"

"Come on."

Toby took off his clothes, made a bundle of them and stepped into the water, holding them over his head.

Clad, pantleg torn, leg bloody, Spike slipped into the river. He scraped his feet in their shoes along the river bottom. He felt for holes before taking each step.

"Come on, Spike."

Toby was in the middle of the river. The water was up to his shoulders. He waited.

From downriver there was a noise. Something had moved in the water. A wet, black triangle appeared in the moonlight on the surface of the water.

There was a rushing noise, the sound of water rushing, the sound of some huge thing rushing through the water at them.

Spike saw the eyes. They were imbecilic, gleaming, wet. He saw the jaws. He saw the massive white teeth separating.

"Oh, Jesus!"

Mouth open, head and body rolling, a shark rushed by him.

It knocked Spike over. His head went underwater.

A few meters beyond where Spike was floundering, the shark suddenly stopped. It had come to the end of its track.

"Jesus!"

Spike regained his footing and stared at it. The shark was bubbling. After a moment, it sank. Spike could feel it moving slowly past him again, going backward underwater.

Through the dark, Toby said calmly, "You must have triggered something with your feet."

"Jesus! Real! I thought it was a real shark!"

"Rivers don't have sharks," Toby said simply. "Except, of course, at Fantazyland."

"Thanks, kid. 'Ppreciate that. Really 'ppreciate it."

"Come on, Spike. Pick your feet up."

By the time Spike reached the riverbank, Toby was nearly dressed in his still dry clothes.

Spike caused a commotion scrambling up the riverbank. A crocodile rose, turned its head toward him, appeared to reach for a bite.

Spike kicked it in the head with his soaked shoe. He slipped in the mud and found himself sitting.

"Good way to make your cut bleed again," Toby commented.

Spike's wound bled again. The blood on his leg was warmer than the river water.

In The Burning House, Toby worked the tourniquet again.

"Should work even better now," Toby said, twisting. "Now that it's wet. Leave it tight until I come back."

"Where you goin'?"

"Outside. I saw a blanket."

In the moonlight, Toby walked up behind the mannequin Indian Chief and said, "Excuse me, sir. We need your blanket." He gave it a tug. It snapped free from around the mannequin's neck.

Spike was a dark form on the floor of the cabin. Toby could hear him shivering.

"Should have taken your clothes off, Spike."

"You shoulda tol' me."

"Take 'em off now. Otherwise the blanket will get wet, too."

Without getting up, Spike struggled out of his clothes. He threw them on the floor and grabbed the blanket over him.

In a minute, Spike said, "Jeez. This is terrible, kid. They got ol' Spike down. You know?"

Fifty-five

"Spike?"

"Yeah, kid?"

Toby was sitting with his back against the inside wall of The Burning House. His arms were around his knees. To him, Spike was a long, dark bulk on the floor. Only Spike's toes, nose and chin were discernible from Toby's view.

"Am I kidnapped?"

"Yeah, kid . . . Toby. I guess you are."

"And you're the kidnapper?"

Shivering: "Yeah. Guess I am. Fac' is. . . . That all right? I mean, that all right with you, Toby?"

"Sure. Just wondering. You know?"

"Sure, kid. Toby. I know. Forget your las' name."

"What?"

"I forget your last name."

"Rinaldi."

"Yeah. Tha's right. Don't take it personal. You know what I mean, kid?"

"Sure."

"I mean. You know. Everybody's gotta make his way. In this world. In this real world out there."

"It's okay."

"Well, frankly . . . fac' is . . . I'm not so sure." He shivered again. "I'm not so sure no more."

". . . And my mother?"

"What about her?"

"She didn't really break her ankle, did she?"

"Naw. How would I know? I never seen your old lady."

"You said so. You said she broke her ankle."

"Well. You see. Toby. Fac' is . . . not everything I say is exactly the truth. You oughta know that."

"How?"

"Well, see. I blow out a lotta air. It's how I get by, if you can dig that. I mean, it's how I do."

"Do what?"

"Get by. If you know what I mean."

"Those other stories, Spike . . ."

"What stories?"

"About rippin' that guy's stomach off. With a knife. With your hands. On the beach."

"Ah, shit. I made that up. You were makin' up stories. Tellin' me stories about some super-creep flyin' through the air in his drawers and a cape, someone stealin' city buses. Whaddaya expect? I told you a story. I made that up. Tearin' off a guy's stomach. I used that story lotsa times. Makes me puke."

"Made me puke."

"Yeah, well, see? That was funny."

"What about the cat?"

"What cat?"

"You ever set fire to a cat?"

"Jeez, no, kid. Naw. I never set fire to no cat. Spin her through the air like that by her tail. I'm no mean guy. Swingin' a cat. When I was a kid in Newark— your age—there was this mean guy on the block, though. I seen him do it. Real mean guy. I hated him. Really hated him. He usta make me toss my cookies. Mean. . . . His name was Spike, see?"

" 'Spike'? Then what's your name?"

"It's Spike, now."

"What was your name? What's your real name?"

". . . Charles."

"Oh. I know someone named Charles."

"Sure you do. See, I hated this guy so much I took the name Spike when I went inta fightin'. Figured if anybody was gonna get his head beat in, better him 'n me. Make sense?"

"Not really."

"See, when I was in reformed school, they made me fight. Taught me a skill: gettin' beat up." Shivering: "I was never any good. They paroled me right to this guy, name of Brian, big promoter he was, full of the manly sport of bleedin'. I spent months fightin' down south. They flew me right outa Newark Airport. Long ways south. Colombia, Venezuela, Bolivia—those places I tol' you about, where they don't speak English too good. Fightin' two, three times a week. Fuckin' face never got time to heal. Every time I fought they gave me twenty-five dollars. Then they'd change it for me into the local money, so I could have a beer, you know? Didn't seem to make any difference whether I won or lost: twenty-five dollars. Always the same twenty-five dollars. I came to recognize the bills. I didn't care. I knew they were poppin' eyes down there. I heard enough about it round the gyms. Brian was always warnin' me. Don't let 'em pop your eye, Spike. I was scared shitless of that. Win or lose: I didn't care. As long as no one popped one of my peepers."

"What do you mean, Spike?"

"You know, during a fight, get a thumb in behind an eyeball. Pop it out."

"Oh."

"Takes a special kinda glove. Less than regulation, Brian called 'em."

"Oh."

"Sure. Fac' is . . . it happened. The night came. Brian was very upset. Sent me home. Newark."

"Oh."

"Didn't hurt so much. Quick, you know? Some reason, less blood comes from the eye like that than usually comes from the nose alla time. Always bein' afraid of its happenin' was much worse. Losin' an eye 'cause some mean guy really popped it out with his thumb on purpose to win a twenty-five dollar fight really rots. You know what I mean? I mean, it's only a fight. Twenty-five dollars. How many beers is that? Jeez. You know what I mean?"

"Yeah. I guess so."

"That's some kinda mean."

"But, Spike, you have been in jail?"

"Yeah. Sure. Twice't Tol' you about that." Shivering: "When I was fourteen, borried a car, didn't know how to drive, smacked it into another car, knocked myself silly. Tweet-tweet. Cops come—there I was, sleeping prince of a jerk. Second time was after I came back from Bolivia. I was starvin', you know. I mean, havin' trouble standin' up I was so hungry. Waited outside a bar one night. Said to myself, next drunk out loses his wallet. Hamburger heaven, here I come! Next drunk out was a plainclothes cop. Bye-bye, Spike. Least the state of New Jersey plugged the hole in my head with a glass marble. For free, too. 'Ppreciated that. I've kept good care of it, too. Before that I had to wear a dollar patch. Like a old pair of pants."

"You mean your glass eye?"

"Yeah. See, kid, in reformed school, you learn to say terrible things about yourself, what you done. Make up big stories, people back off. Stay outa your pants. Fac' is, I'm mostly good at takin' stories from the newspapers, then makin' 'em up about myself. I make 'em real, know what I mean? What I do, see, see, is I stand around the bars in Newark, some of 'em, tellin' stories. I guess I look like I should be believed. This face . . . People believe me, see? I scare 'em shitless. Then, every once't in a while someone comes up to me, says, 'Spike, there's this guy needs his legs broken, his head beat in, his house torched, car kaboomed.'

And I say, 'Sure, how much?' real easy, just like that, as if I'm beatin' up on so many people I'll have difficulty fittin' one more into my busy schedule. I allus take half up front. Cash money. I'm no dope."

"Then do you do it?"

"Do what?"

"Beat up on somebody?"

"Shit, no. I move on to another bar. There's lotsa bars in Newark."

"Don't they come after you? They gave you money. Why don't they beat you up?"

"If they weren't so chickenshit about beatin' people up themselves, they wouldna hired me. Right? What money? Most I ever took, twenty dollars, fifty, once't a C-note. Anyhow, they're all too scared o' me! Scared shitless. This face o' mine. . . . If I ever saw 'em again, I'd say, 'Oh, yeah. I forgot. Been busy. I'll get to it next week.' See? Like that. A little business."

For a while they both sat in the dark, listening to Spike's teeth chattering.

Then Toby asked, "So how come you kidnapped me?"

"Aw, that was nothin'," Spike said. "Just doin' a friend a favor."

"Nice friend," Toby said. "Nice favor."

"Aw, don't go all snotty on me, kid. Don't take it personal. Ain't you never done a friend a favor?"

"Yes," Toby said.

"Well, tha's what I was doin'. I was doin' a friend a favor. Name o' Donny Dubrowski. Swell guy. You'd like him, kid. Knew him in prison, up in Attica. He was in for this and that. Only, he was smart, see? None of this fightin' shit for him. He lifted weights. Worked out real hard. You know, developed his body? He got as strong as a horse. Two horses maybe. Body building is a smart sport. Nobody hits ya. Nobody pulls your eye out. Only, there you are lookin' like you could beat up the whole world with one twitch of a deltoid."

"What's a deltoid?"

"Anyway, Donny got sprung seven, eight months ago. We saw each other sometimes. I didn't exactly know what he was doin', exactly, but, fact' is, he always had money in his jeans. He knew the stories I was tellin' in the bars were full of shit. Jus' my way of doin' business. I'd tol' the same kinda stories up in Attica. To keep guys off'n me.

"Then just the other day, like, last week, Donny come to me and ast me to do him a favor. One look at him . . . 'Aw, Donny,' I said. 'You got a snootful.' "

"What's a snootful?"

"He'd climbed the ladder, kid."

"What ladder?"

"He was flyin' without wings. Seems someone gived him a job to do—kidnappin' you—and Donny had temporarily messed up his head. He knew he could come down, though. Just take time."

"I don't understand you, Spike. What was wrong with your friend?"

Shivering: "He was sick, kid. Had the flu."

"Oh."

"So he ast me if I'd stand in for him while he got better. He said, 'How'd you like a ride to California on an airplane?' I said, 'Sure.' He said, 'Pick up this kid at the airport—that's you, Toby—and he tol' me how, and what to say, and give me this special jacket to wear, and he gived me two thousand bucks. Think of it! Two thousand of 'em, all in my pocket at the same time, me owin' nobody.

"But I owed Donny I do this job for him. So I did it. And tha's a fac'. You saw me do it, dincha, Toby?"

"Yeah."

"I did a good job kidnappin' you, too, dinnin' I?"

"Guess so."

"Sure I did."

"So what happened to your friend, Spike?"

"Tha's the fac' I dunno. See, I suppost to fly out here with you, lyin' to you all the way, grab a car, drive you to that fancy Dan hotel, the Fairmont, then call Donny for further instructions, he said."

"So what happened? What happened when you called him?"

"He wasn't home."

Toby ran his finger along the scratch on his forehead. He had discovered the cut after the men had shot at him and Spike. He figured his forehead had been glazed by a wood chip, or a bullet.

Spike shivered. "He never answered the phone. Fac' is, he never answered the phone."

"He must be real sick," Toby said.

"Must be," Spike agreed.

"Could your friend be dead of the flu, Spike?"

"I dunno, kid. Could be."

Toby said, "Good night, Spike."

He stretched out along the wall of The Burning House.

"Toby?"

"Yeah?"

"You want the blanket?"

"No, thanks. My clothes are dry."

"Sorry you ain't got no pajamas. I know how you like 'em."

"That's okay," Toby said. "I'm not in bed."

Shivering: "Jeez, I thought that shark was real. Jus' for a minute, there. . . ."

Fifty-six

"Wake up, Spike! Come on! Wake up! I found a whole world, with nobody in it!"

Kneeling over him, Toby was shaking Spike's shoulder.

Spike opened his eyes. His right eye focused on the door of The Burning House. It was just after dawn. There was a wind.

"Look!" Toby moved to the back corner of the cabin. There was a thin railing in a half circle. "Stairs. We didn't see them last night. I've already been down, on an explore. There's a big tunnel down there. I smelled food. Bread cooking. Come on!"

He returned and pulled the blanket off Spike.

"Sorry," Toby said. "Forgot you're naked."

Spike sat up and looked at the floor near his leg. There was wet blood. "I been leakin'," Spike said.

"Not much."

"I feel bushed."

"We'll eat," Toby said brightly.

"I need blood. God. I seen more of my own blood than any other dude alive."

Toby picked up Spike's trousers. "They're still damp. Should have hung them up."

"You didn't tell me."

"Let's go."

"No, I can't move, kid. They've really got Spike down this time."

Toby handed Spike his shirt. "Put it on."

Spike said, "Not going anywhere." He put on his clammy shirt.

Toby forced Spike's sticky socks on his feet.

From the front of the cabin there was a single quiet

pop. Suddenly, the front of the cabin, near the window and door, was a mass of shooting, licking, whooshing flames.

"Jesus Christ!"

"Asbestos," Toby said. "Can't burn, remember?"

"Like hell!" Spike was up, hopping around trying to pull on his trousers.

Toby's head was visible at the top of the stairwell. "Must be an automatic pilot light," he commented.

"Hot as hell!"

"Come on, then."

Spike hobbled after Toby down the long, circular iron staircase. By the time he reached the bottom, Toby had opened the door to the tunnel.

Spike looked to his right and his left along the corridor lit dimly by the inset-base lights.

"I'll be a goose's rear end. So that's how they run this place! What a basement!"

Toby let the door close. The sign on it said: Maintenance BURNING HOUSE RED CARD EMPLOYEES ONLY.

"Smell food?" Toby asked.

"Fac' is, I do. Yes, I do."

They went along the corridor slowly. Spike stayed near the right wall, putting his hand out to it frequently.

They followed their noses to the large, still darkened employees' cafeteria. In the dim light from the corridor, they found the serving counters and went behind them. Most were bare. On one near the cash registers there were some sandwiches wrapped in cellophane and some half-pint cartons of milk.

They stood in the dark and munched.

"What did you get?" Toby asked.

"Roas' beef."

"I got tuna. . . . What did you get this time?"

"Roas' beef."

"I did, too."

The great fluorescent ceiling lights began to flicker on in waves.

A man in a white apron stood in the kitchen door holding a large spoon.

"Hey!" he said.

Toby dropped his sandwich. "Let's go!"

"Nice to know ya," Spike said.

They dodged around the counter and ran through the dining area.

"Hey, you! Come back here!"

They turned left down the corridor and kept running.

Toby looked back.

The cook was standing in the middle of the corridor. "HEY!"

Toby pushed limping Spike around a corner into another corridor that ran to the left.

Fifty-seven

Christina felt her feet were buried in hot sand.

She woke up, sat up and looked at them. She was on a couch in the Health Office.

She couldn't see her feet very well in the semidark, but her fingers told her how swollen and lacerated they were.

Standing on them was agony.

There was a lamp on the desk. She snapped it on.

On the wall beside the desk was a medicine cabinet with a glass front. It was locked. She broke the glass with a desk stapler. Inside were liquid antiseptics, salves, ointments. Sitting in the desk chair, she poured almost everything she could find onto her feet, one after the other, rubbing them as hard as she could stand. The pain and the pleasure went up the back of her legs to the back of her head.

Under the typewriter was a pair of nurse's white shoes. Gingerly, she tried one on. It was blissfully loose.

Removing the shoe, she wrapped both feet in Ace bandages she found in the medicine cabinet. Then she put the shoes on and laced them tight. She stood up. It would be possible to walk. She would walk. She snapped out the desk light and opened the door.

Fifty-eight

Colonel Turnbull was under the bench in The Victorian Railroad Station, hands folded across his chest, suit coat bunched under his head, finally asleep.

"Colonel?"

"Shut up."

Monks was over him, on one knee.

"Shut your face."

"People around here," Monks said softly. "Employees arriving. Better move."

"I said, *Shut up!*"

Reaching around, Turnbull used the edge of the bench to pull himself into a sitting position. He worked his way up to his feet.

"Rinaldi," Turnbull said. Coughing, he corkscrewed phlegm out of his chest and spat it on the railroad station's floor.

"Shh," Monks said. He retrieved the Colonel's coat from under the bench.

"There's an elevator in there." Monks held the Colonel's coat. "It goes down somewhere."

The other two men was standing in the stationmaster's office. The elevator door was open.

His eyes red, his hands shaking, Turnbull stepped into the elevator.

Fifty-nine

Item 1: Dodge Aspen Stationwagon left in main parking lot last Saturday P.M. identified by Nevada Police as stolen. Owner notified. Will pick up Wednesday. Name of Gotlieb.

Item 2: Pink Card Employee (cook) José Jones reported seven twenty A.M. two persons in or near employees' cafeteria: man, about thirty, torn trousers, limping; boy, about ten, white shorts, blue shirt; together.

Item 3: Pink Card Employee (aquamaid) Kathy Runson reported eight-three A.M. bikini top missing from locker third time in week.

Item. 4: Black Card Employee (watchman) Grieves reported eight-thirty A.M. meeting Black Card Employee (watchman) Billy Joe Carfer on path near Future Transport Rocket at one-fifteen A.M. driving patrol vehicle erratically. Not responsive when spoken to. Carfer, age twenty-two, is known to have an interest in art.

Item 5: White Card Employee (nurse) Lydia Kozol reported eight-thirty A.M. office medicine chest broken into, salves, bandages missing. Also missing were her shoes.

Item. 6: Disturbance reported in aquamaids' locker room eight-forty-seven A.M. Pink Card Employee Kathy Runson sent to Personnel.

Chief Constable Drew Keosian had his hand on his desk telephone before he finished reading the morning report.

Joe Grady, his second-in-command (Mobile Unit), picked up.

"Read the morning report yet, Joe?"

"Yeah. That Kathy Runson sounds like a hot ticket. What's she got the other aquamaids haven't got? That's what I want to know."

Keosian had never been keen on indecent reference. In his job, he had to accept a certain amount of it.

"Two men and a boy in Fantazyland Under. At dawn. One man possibly wounded."

Drew Keosian had not slept well. He had tried to conceptualize how there could have been a real shooting incident in Wild West City—how two men could possibly have shot into that crowd without hitting anybody. He had told himself it couldn't have happened.

"Yeah."

"And I doubt either the man or the boy stole Nurse Kozol's shoes."

"Or Kathy Runson's bikini top. . . ."

"Put half the available constables into the Underground. Tell them what they're looking for. I'll be going right down myself."

"Yes, sir."

"And, Joe, this character, Item Four, Billy Joe Carfer, watchman?"

"Yes, sir?"

"Fire him."

"Yes, sir."

Drew put the telephone receiver back on its yoke. From his desk drawer he took a .38 caliber handgun.

He checked it quickly. Standing up, he dropped it in his pants pocket.

Leaving his office, crossing to the elevator, he reminded himself, *Even in Eden, the snakes. . . .*

Sixty

In the dim light of the main corridor of the tunnel there were four people.

Christina was aware that far up the corridor a man was limping away from her. She had no idea who he was. More to her interest, behind her down the corridor was the tall man in the gray suit she had last seen asleep in the chair. *I'm seeing rather too much of him,* she thought. Behind him, a constable had stepped into the corridor. He was standing still, looking in her direction.

Christina looked back and forth.

Around a corner came a monkey wearing a red hat. It was riding a green unicycle. Over its shoulder it carried a yellow umbrella.

The monkey chattered at Christina insistently. In warning? In anger?

The walls echoed the monkey's chatter.

Suddenly, there was light. Everywhere. Blinding light. It poured from the tops of both walls. Triangled behind glass between walls and ceilings were fluorescent lights.

The tall man in the gray suit shouted, "Mullins!"

On top of his echo the constable shouted, "Hey! Freeze!"

Chattering nervously, the monkey made a perfect U-turn on its unicycle. Furiously, it pedaled up the corridor and around a corner.

Christina shouted, "What's happening?"

Pale eyes staring, the tall man in the gray suit strided quickly past her.

The constable flung off his helmet and ran after him. His nightstick bounced against his leg.

The man with the limp had disappeared.

Christina yelled after the constable, "What's happening?"

In the corridor remained only the echo of her own voice.

Sixty-one

Toby, walking ahead of Spike in the tunnel, had just turned a corner. Behind him, instead of Spike, came a monkey on a unicycle, shaking its fist. It rode in a circle around Toby and tried to hit him over the head with an umbrella.

"Hey, lay off!" Toby said.

As the lights in the corridor came on, the monkey rode away, looking back at him angrily.

From around the corner came the sound of shouting. A woman's voice was shouting a question. A man's voice was shouting a statement, or a name. The edges of the voices were blurred by the hard tunnel walls.

Spike came around the corner, favoring his wounded leg. He was moving fast.

"Let's go," Spike said. "Go, go!"

*

They went.

Spike dragged his leg after him. He kept his hand behind his thigh to continue pushing his leg forward. He was still losing blood. His face was drained, white.

Leading, Toby decided their direction.

"Come on, Spike. In here!"

"Aw, shut up, ya little punk."

"Through here, Spike! Hurry up!"

"Punk kid. I'm hurryin'!"

They went up an elevator marked, RED CARD EMPLOYEES ONLY.

Just after the elevator door closed behind them,

they discovered they were in the target area of a shooting gallery.

"Aw, shit!" Spike dropped to all fours. Rifle pellets shot over their heads and thwacked against a thick mat. "Now everybody's shootin' at ol' Spike!"

They crawled through a cable tunnel and dropped into a room full of loud, huge, hot machinery.

"Wait a minute, Toby! Gotta sit down. Gotta rest. All my blood leaked out, ya know. . . ."

"Too noisy here," Toby shouted.

"Gimme a chance, willya, kid?"

Spike followed him.

Underground, they went along iron scaffolding. Deep pits of machinery—humming, hissing, thumping, pumping machinery—yawned below them. Toby ran from pit to pit. Waiting for Spike, he looked down at the machinery, studying it. The machines were enormous, but intricate.

Spike worked his way along the scaffold, averting his eyes from everything below him. He kept both hands on the thin railing.

"Wow!" Toby said. "Look at that!"

"Yeah, yeah, kid. You look at it."

*

They went through various twists and turns of a tunnel not big enough for a horse. An organ was screeching shrill, spine-tingling music. It reverberated from the walls, ceiling, floor.

"Hey, Spike! Look at this!"

Toby had found a small, narrow, green-tinted window in the wall. It took Spike's eye a moment to adjust.

He was looking into the living room of Spooky House. An open coffin was at one side of the room.

The corpse was a young lady. Her hands were around the stem of a rose upon her breast. At the coffin's foot was a lit candle. A flour-faced hag, a ghost, long white hair down the back of her long nightgown, passed through the room. The arm of a standing suit of armor clanked a chain.

And the organ screeched.

The tourists smiled and laughed and applauded and took pictures.

In the middle of the crowd were the two gunmen who had shot at Spike and Toby the day before. With them was a third man—a heavy man in a bulky, rough suit. Each was looking around and up and down the walls in a far more methodical manner than were the tourists.

"Hey, Spike!" Toby punched him in the arm. "Spooky House. Remember? We're in the walls of Spooky House. Cool, huh?"

Spike looked away. Something in his stomach was bothering him.

"Yeah," he said. "Cool. I think we better keep movin', kid."

"Don't you want to rest? I want to watch the people be scared."

Spike limped on. "You can watch me."

*

Toby was the first up a metal ladder. At the top, he pushed open a trap door and pulled himself through. In this tunnel there was a railroad track. He stood in the middle of it.

A railroad train was heading straight for him. Its headlight was piercing. The whistle was urgent, shrill.

"Boo!" Toby said to it. "You'll never hit me!"

He helped Spike through the trap door.

"Look at this, Spike. Remember that ride we were

on? You go through the tunnel and you think a train is going to hit you and you get right up to it and it's only an illusion and suddenly it isn't there anymore? We're there! I mean, here. There's the train."

Spike stood on the track.

"You forgot somethin', Toby."

"What?"

The structure beneath their feet was trembling.

"A train goes through here. Punk kid! The one we were on."

"Oh, yeah," Toby said. "I forgot."

He had dropped the trap door.

A train of wagonettes came around the curve. Aboard were tourists—so many white arms and faces—screaming and laughing.

Spike said, "Shit!"

He grabbed Toby's shoulder and pulled him against the wall.

The tourists swayed by them, eyes gleaming, mouths open, hair flying, row after row, screaming at the illusion they were about to be hit by an oncoming train.

The eyes of one girl fell on Toby. Her head snapped around. She looked at him again.

With a final, deafening hoot, the oncoming train disappeared.

The train of wagonettes clattered on.

The tourists shrieked away.

Sixty-two

We're in The Hat. We're in The Hat, Toby sang to himself. *We're in The Hat. And Spike doesn't know it.*

They had returned to the main tunnels of Fantazyland Underground. Immediately, Toby smelled food. They walked a short way along the sidewalk.

Spike stopped. He leaned his hand against the wall. He lifted his damaged leg as if kicking it slowly and looked at his foot.

"It's all swole," he said.

Keeping his weight off his foot, Spike leaned his back against the wall. In that light, Toby thought Spike looked as white as the girl in the coffin in Spooky House. Even whiter. As white as the ghost.

"People will come along here," Toby warned.

"Like who?" Spike asked. "Ghosts. Sharks. Railroad trains. What else? Jeez, I dunno." He took a deep breath. "I dunno, kid."

Toby shrugged. "People," he said.

Spike snorted, coughed. " 'People,' " he said.

He rubbed his good eye.

"That's a laugh. 'People.' Tell me another."

Facing Spike, Toby was balancing himself on the sidewalk's curb.

Toby said, "Like the two guys who shot at us yesterday. In Wild West City."

"Them two. They shoulda been taken out with the garbage."

Quietly, Toby said, "They weren't. I'm looking at them."

Spike's head snapped up. "You're lookin' at 'em?"

"Yeah."

"Where?"

Without moving his head, Toby said, "They're coming down the corridor. To my left."

"Yeah? No foolin'."

"No foolin'."

"They see you?"

"Sure, they see me."

"They got guns?"

"Suppose so."

"Why aren't they shootin' at ya?"

"I'm just a kid. Grown-ups can't tell kids apart."

"It's me they'll shoot at. Right?"

Toby said, "I expect so."

"Yeah? So whadda we do? My back's against the wall. See?"

"There's an elevator right next to you."

"Yeah? So there is."

"Press the button."

The sign on the elevator said, DOUBLE RED CARD EMPLOYEES ONLY. NO OTHER ADMITTANCE.

"Guess what, Spike? They see you."

The elevator door opened.

Spike looked around.

"It is them same guys!"

They got into the elevator. Toby pushed the button.

The two men were loping down the corridor toward them.

The elevator door closed and the car shot upward in a surprising, ear-cracking rush. It rose for a fairly long time.

We're in The Hat. We're in The Hat.

"No stops," Spike said.

*

The elevator door slid open.

Spike looked out. His working eye widened.

"Oh, Lord," he said. "Look where we are."

"Yeah," Toby said. "Top of The Hat."

"Oh, no."

"Can't go back down in the elevator, Spike."

Spike limped off the elevator. "Must be some other way down."

There was a heavy mesh fence between them and the platform where the tourists stood in line. The front of the line fed people into the small, brightly painted gondolas.

When a gondola had a party of two or four in it, it would slip down the track and fall onto the rail outside The Hat. Instantly, the people would begin screaming. They would appear against the sky for only a moment before they would drop down to the left, out of sight.

Music was playing.

Roundsy, roundsy . . .

Downsy, downsy . . .

Toby and Spike were on the maintenance men's side of the mesh fence.

A man appeared against the other side. Though it was softened by the fence, Toby thought the man's face dreadful. It was fat and broken with lines and bumps. The red eyes were staring at him.

"Are you Tobias Rinaldi?"

"Yes, sir."

"Well, Tobias Rinaldi, I'm your uncle." The man reached inside his suit coat. "Augustus Turnbull. And I'm going to kill you. And then your mother. And then your precious father!"

Toby sidled along the fence to his left, toward daylight. He felt wind.

There was a ledge. It was black, smooth plastic. Like a lip, it curved outward and downward.

Behind him, Turnbull shouted, "Mullins!"

Toby stepped onto the ledge. From what he could see, it went around the outside of The Hat.

Roundsy, roundsy . . .

A gondola dropped onto the track. The ledge began to vibrate. The tourists were screaming in their own fright.

Toby tried to jump back, off the ledge. The vibration was too much. He had already been shaken half a meter down the ledge.

The gondola was pirouetting in front of Toby. The people's faces looked truly frightened.

To his right, another gondola dropped onto the track.

Somewhere a voice shouted, "There's a kid out there!"

Toby sat down. Whatever traction the soles of his sneakers had given him he lost. The seat of his shorts gave him none. The vibration of the ledge was banging up his spinal column. His teeth were chattering.

The second gondola was pirouetting in the air in front of him. The tourists were laughing. One, who was not laughing, was trying to point to him.

Roundsy, roundsy . . .

Toby's feet went over the edge. He tried to hold himself back with the flat of his hands. He fell forward. Below him, all Fantazyland moved, tilted. Wind shouted in his ears.

His fingers grabbed the outside gondola track. He was hanging from the rail by his fingers. He held on, dangled in space.

The track began to shake. Toby looked up. A yellow gondola had dropped onto the track. It would run over his fingers.

Toby let go.

Downsy, downsy . . .

Below him, Fantazyland zoomed closer.

"Ow!"

His mouth banged shut. His knees, the small of his back, his neck jolted. His feet had landed on something. He tried to steady himself. The wind helped. He bent his knees and put out his hands and let himself down.

Toby was well outside The Hat, outside the gondola track. He was on a black guard rail.

Lying on it, he hugged it with his arms and legs. Fantazyland was still far below him. The roofs were many colors and many shapes. The paths seemed aimless. People looked like little bugs. The wind filled his ears, bringing snatches of carousel music. He could hear the lovely, awful noise of the air-cushion boat on the lake.

Then he heard the gondola track rattling.

Toby looked up.

A red gondola was coming. One man was in it. Under his flapping jacket he wore an Uncle Whimsy T-shirt. The man's arm was reaching out of the gondola at him.

Toby put out his left hand for the man to grab.

But instead, he felt the man's hand against his ribs . . . pushing!

Toby held onto the rail tight, with both arms.

The gondola was gone.

Toby was panting. The wind made his lips flap.

A sudden melody blew in from the carousel. He recognized *Waltzing Matilda*. He had heard that song years ago when he had gone with his parents and His Majesty to some big, sunny country where all the people were big and sunburned and laughed loud and grabbed him and hugged him.

At the sound of the track rattling, he looked up again. A green gondola was coming.

Augustus. He said his name was Augustus. Colonel Augustus Something. Why did he say he was my knuckle?

Colonel Augustus Turnbull was in the gondola. He was aiming a pistol at Toby. He was coming very close. The hole in the pistol's barrel was a perfect circle.

The gondola spun the man around.

The gun went off.

Toby turned his head. He was looking outward at the sky. He looked down. Fantazyland swayed, like a rug moving under his feet.

He shot The Hat! Colonel Augustus Something-or-other shot Uncle Whimsy's Hat!

"TOBY?"

The next gondola was pink. Spike was standing up in it, waving both his arms.

"Wake up, punk! Le's go! Reach out here. Come on! Le go that thing!"

Sitting up a little, keeping both legs wrapped around the guard rail, Toby sent his arms toward Spike.

Spike yelled, "Grab me! Lean in. Come on, le's go!"

The inside of Toby's legs got scraped. His head was moving. He closed his eyes. There was a massive hand on each side of his rib cage. The back of his head bounced on something metallic.

He looked up. He was on the floor of the gondola. The sky above him was spinning. Spike's head was going in a circle. Spike's hand was on Toby's bare stomach.

The sky stopped spinning. Spike's head straightened. The muscles in his neck were bulging. Both his hands grabbed the safety bar.

They were moving straight ahead.

The gondola was gathering speed.

"You know, kid . . ." The world went dark. " . . . this ain't percisely my favorite ride. . . ."

Sixty-three

Christina was looking down from a scaffold into what appeared to be a sixteenth-century banquet hall. Two men dressed as cavaliers, lace collars and cuffs, plumed hats, were dueling with swords. They jumped onto the banquet table, leaped over a soup tureen, kicked aside a roast pig. . . .

The tourists smiled and laughed and applauded and took pictures.

She examined the crowd carefully.

No Toby.

In the crowd there were three boys of about his age. One was blond and overweight and hot. He looked like an apple being baked. One was so skinny his knees looked like doorknobs. The third glowed. She thought he looked rather like Toby.

How many small boys had she seen the last few days that looked something like Toby . . . ? It was a phenomenon with which she was familiar. Missing Toby so much, frequently in a street in New York, in a department store, passing Central Park in the car, Christina would catch her breath at the sight of a boy for a fraction of a second she would think was Toby. For a long moment then, she would be sad at the thought of Toby in school in New Hampshire, at a sailing camp on Cape Cod—being somewhere, anywhere away from her. The last days, in the airport, in the streets, at Fantazyland, the phenomenon of seeing someone who was like Toby, who she wanted to believe was Toby, had been frequent. The psychological phenomenon was cruel.

In the white shoes, Christina had plodded along the main Underground tunnel corridor. The constable, the man in the long overcoat, the limping man—even the chattering monkey—had disappeared.

Wanting to get out, back to the surface of the earth, Christina took elevators.

The first brought her to the inside of a mammoth music box. The din it made was horrible. *The flowers that bloom in the spring, tra la* . . . She knew she was in Princess Daphne's Flower Palace.

She did not know where she was when the door of the second elevator opened. She was facing a green wall. Immediately, a five-foot duck waddled onto the elevator. It stood beside her, looking sideways at her curiously. Silently, Christina rode the elevator down again with the duck.

The third elevator brought her into the stomach of a whale. She looked through a window in the whale's side. Pilot fish dangled on barely visible wires. A submarine glided through the murky water.

She finally went through an ordinary door, up a steep iron ladder and along a scaffold. At least from there she had seen some children, even if Toby wasn't among them.

The metal scaffold began to quiver. At about the pace of a heartbeat. Footsteps. She looked ahead through the gloom. The tall, skinny man in the gray suit appeared in the distance, walking toward her.

Quietly, she moved in the opposite direction.

Below her another room, oddly lit, opened up. She looked over the railing down into it.

A long rope swung ponderously back and forth. At the end of it gleamed a razor-shap pendulum. Around the room were guillotines of various sizes and styles. One after the other, the blades would rise slowly, then fall with a horrendous clash.

Moving back and forth in the room in a frightening, lurching manner was a huge wooden barrel. It turned slowly as it moved back and forth, up and down. Long, flashing knives stuck out of it at every angle, from every direction. Looking at it, Christina became nauseous.

This must be The Hall of Knives. Behind a rope, tourists stood. For once, they looked solemn, surrounded as they were by machines of death.

Someone grabbed the hair at the back of Christina's head, pulled her back, roughly twisted her head around.

Turnbull's face was an inch from hers. The veins in his eyes bulged.

"Christina . . . Finch . . . Rinaldi!" The last word struck her in the face with spittle. He yanked her hair harder. "Where is the boy?"

"Stop!"

"You don't have the boy, do you?"

"No! Stop!"

"You don't know where the boy is, do you?"

"No. No, I don't!"

"But I have you, haven't I? . . . Christina Rinaldi."

Holding on to her hair, he pulled her head back, twisting her neck.

"I have you . . . and I shall have the little bastard . . . won't I?"

Long, bony white fingers appeared on Turnbull's shoulders.

Turnbull looked around.

The face of the tall man in the gray suit was paper white. In the dim light, the pupils of his eyes were almost colorless.

Turnbull let go of Christina's hair. He turned around to face the man. They all stood close together on the narrow scaffold. Christina's back was against the thin metal railing.

"Yes, Simon?" Turnbull said softly. "What do you want?"

"I need the woman, Gus." Cord's tone was as reasonable as a teacher explaining geometry. "I need the boy. Only another few hours."

"Another few hours for you to mess up again, Cord? For me to lose them both?"

"Gus—"

"No!" Turnbull roared. "I've shit in this bed! If they don't die, and die now . . ." Holding his hands before his chest, he tightened his fingers as if squeezing tennis balls. " . . . I've yet to get *precious Teodoro.* . . ."

"Another few hours, Gus." Cord's pale eyes flickered at Christina. "Then you can waste the whole family, all we care."

Turnbull swung his fist. He hit Cord on the jaw.

Then his fingers dug into Christina's neck. The balls of his thumbs pressed into her throat.

She tried to raise her knee, but Turnbull was too close.

There was a flash of white over Turnbull's shoulder as Cord chopped him in the neck.

Turnbull let go of Christina.

"Gus, you're insane," Cord said conversationally.

Cord slammed the side of his hand against Turnbull's throat.

Turnbull staggered forward. He drew his other hand back to his shoulder to swing at Cord.

Cord laced his fingers together and put them against Turnbull's face. He stepped beside Turnbull and threw his hips against Turnbull's and pushed.

Turnbull's feet rose from the scaffold. Blood was dribbling from his nose and mouth.

Cord, sideways to the railing, had all his weight on one foot.

Immediately, impulsively, instinctively, Christina jumped and hit Cord's near shoulder with both hands. She put her full weight into the blow. Cord's waist was well above the railing, his head already on the other side.

Cord turned his face to Christina. He knew he was falling. The expression on his face was totally indifferent.

Christina's left hand clutched the railing. From below there was loud, delighted screaming.

She looked over the railing. Both men had landed on the twirling barrel of knives.

Turnbull was spreadeagled on his back. The knives that protruded from his stomach glistened with blood.

Cord had landed on his stomach. Knives pierced his shoulder, his chest, his back, one leg.

The barrel lurched round and round, back and forth, up and down, rotating the bodies. Blood dripped onto the floor in crazy patterns.

The tourists smiled and laughed and applauded and took pictures.

Sixty-four

"Ma'am, what are you doing here?"

For the moment, Christina could not answer. She was in the main corridor of Fantazyland's Underground again. All the lights were on. She could not remember how she got there. Had she ever left?

She pressed the heel of her hand against her temple. She remembered kneeling on some iron rungs . . . the scaffold . . . vomiting . . . dry wretching. Then wanting to go somewhere, anywhere, walking. . . .

She looked around the walls and ceiling of the brightly lit tunnel.

There was a constable standing before her. His face was surprisingly tanned, for that handlebar mustache, that bobby's helmet. There was a patrol vehicle standing in the middle of the corridor. There was another man, dressed in a light sports jacket. He had his hand on her arm.

"My name is Drew Keosian," he said. "I work here at Fantazyland. I want to help you."

Far up the corridor, a man limped around the corner. One of his pant legs looked wet, adhered to his leg.

Behind him loped a small boy. White shorts, blue jersey. . . .

"Oh, my God," Christina said.

Keosian looked around.

"Toby!"

He looked straight at his mother.

What is he doing? What is Toby doing?

The boy put his hands on the man's back, turned him around and pushed him. He hurried the man back around the corner, out of sight.

"Toby!" Christina screamed again.

Keosian and the constable jumped onto the patrol vehicle. The cart accelerated instantly, quietly.

Its brake lights flashed as it went around the corner.

*

Again, Christina was alone in the corridor.

Toby. . . . What is wrong with Toby . . . ?

As well as she could on her damaged feet, Christina ran along the corridor.

He saw me. . . . I know he saw me. . . . He heard me. . . . I know he did. Toby! As she hurried along, Christina tried to clear her eyes of tears. She turned the corner. She looked both ways.

There was no one at all in sight.

A little more slowly, trying to even out her breathing, trying to dry her face, Christina walked. The bandages in her shoes were wet with blood. Her feet slipped in the shoes.

At the next intersection, instead of turning left, Christina crossed the corridor and took the tunnel to the right.

A five-foot beaver, dragging its tail on the floor, hurried past her.

Then she heard Toby's voice. He sounded so casual, as if he were trying to wake her up.

"Hey, Mom?"

Christina spun around, slipping in the big white shoes.

Toby stood against the wall, grinning. Next to him was a door marked, COSTUMES.

All the breath went out of her.

"Where you been, Mom?"

She grabbed him. She folded him into her arms.

"What's the matter with your feet? Did you really break your ankles?"

"Toby, Toby, Toby. . . ."

"Ma'am? Hey, you! Ma'am! Miss!"

A constable down the corridor was waving his arm at them as he jogged toward them. "Wait a minute, miss!"

From under her breasts, Toby looked up at his mother, smiled and said, "Come on!"

He took Christina by the arm and pulled her a few steps. He pushed a button on the wall.

A door slid open.

"In here." He pulled her in. Grinning, he said, "Up?"

He pushed another button. The elevator door closed.

Christina held Toby close to her. She pressed his body against hers.

Then, like a mother cat, she took his hair in her mouth. She put her wet cheeks against the top of his head and kissed it again and again.

"Toby, Toby, Toby, Toby, Toby," she said. "Oh, Toby, Toby, Toby, Toby. . . ."

Sixty-five

"Mr. Ambassador? I know you asked not to be disturbed at all, but Mrs. Rinaldi is on line 253. She says it is urgent."

At his desk, Ambassador Teodoro Rinaldi looked around his office at his staff. They sat with papers in their laps, pens in their hands. The eyes of each of them had fallen at the sound of Sylvia Menninges's voice over the intercom.

He looked at his watch. In two hours he was scheduled to stand before the assembled delegates to the United Nations and submit Resolution 1176R.

The button on line 253 was flashing. Teddy put his hand on the receiver.

He was not sure that he wanted to, or could, talk to Christina just then. It was her right; it was her need to ask him what he had decided.

That afternoon Teddy had received a coldly worded directive from the King ordéring him to submit Resolution 1176R.

Two hours before he was to deliver the speech, Ambassador Teodoro Rinaldi had decided nothing. He had simply continued operating as well as he could, upon the basic principle of diplomacy: *keep all options open as long as possible*. Many, many times he had learned the greatest mistake was in making a decision before it had to be made. Several times in his professional career he had believed he had all the facts necessary, all the facts available, to make a decision, hesitated just a moment longer and been surprised by a new fact, totally unexpected, that changed his decision totally. A nervy game few diplomats played well, others seemed not to understand.

Pretending they were not there—not hearing, seeing—his staff, in this final meeting two hours before the culmination of all their work, hopes, just before he was expected to offer a masterwork of diplomacy to create a new economic sanity, a new, essential peace guarantee, for their nation, their people, their homes, for the world, sat there, eyes on their laps, doodling on pads. They were aware of his hesitation in answering the phone.

Urgent? If there was bad news about Toby, the Ambassador was certain he couldn't assimilate it, accept it; he couldn't take it.

He had better hear it.

Teddy put the receiver to his ear. "Christina?"

"Hi, Dad."

The Ambassador looked around at his staff, around the room at the tops of their heads.

"Toby?"

Suddenly, he was seeing faces in his office. Faces. Not tops of heads.

"Toby! Are you all right?"

"Sure."

"Your mother with you?"

"Sure."

The faces were beaming.

"Is she all right?"

"Her feet hurt."

"What's wrong with her feet?"

"She walks like one of those ducks out here. She waddles."

"Where are you?"

"Fantazyland. It's a great place, Dad."

"Look." Teddy swallowed. "Don't see everything without me. I'm coming out. In a couple of days. Join you. We'll want to see some of it together."

"I've seen about all of it, Dad. I can show you. I even know how most things work."

Teddy felt he had to hang up. Soon. He had not many moments of control left. "Toby? Ask your mother to call me. Tonight. She knows when and where."

"Okay."

"I'll see you soon, Toby. Wednesday. Thursday at the latest."

"Okay."

Teddy replaced the receiver. He looked around his office—at the faces of the people in his office.

"Well," he said. "Toby seems to have made it to Fantazyland."

Ria's eyes were bathed in tears. She was grinning.

"Excuse me." Teddy stood up. "A moment."

He went into his bathroom and closed the door.

○

In his office, his staff sat silently.

Ria blew her nose.

Through the bathroom door they could hear the tap water splashing hard into the basin.

Then they heard another sound—frightening, until they recognized it.

They did not look at each other. Of course, they were embarrassed.

Finally, the final-draft speech writer said, "It seems His Excellency, the Ambassador, is blubbering in the bathroom."

Ria Marti closed her notebook.

She said, "I think this meeting is over."

Sixty-six

There was only one constable at the main gate of Fantazyland. Because of Christina's feet, she and Toby were moving slowly. The constable paid them no particular attention. They had washed their hands and faces, tried to clean their clothes. Fantazyland constables were not very concerned with people who were leaving. Just those who were entering.

Holding his mother's hand, Toby had plenty of time to look around. Of course he looked back at Uncle Whimsy's Hat. From here, the side of the mountainous, black Stovepipe Hat seemed absolutely smooth. The bright-colored gondolas popping out of its top seemed not big enough to carry ants. To its left were the stone turrets of Princess Daphne's Flower Castle.

In the turn-of-the-century square itself, the Flags of All Nations atop the buildings were straight out in the wind. The Firemen's Band was playing, *Glory, Glory hallelujah* . . .

A voice said, "Toby. . . ."

Toby saw no one he recognized. Tourists wandered around. There was the constable; the girl dressed as Princess Daphne, handing flowers to little girls; a sad-faced clown, his white-painted lips curving down; an upright turtle, five and a half feet tall. . . .

"Hey, Toby. . . ."

Toby looked closely at the clown. His makeup didn't seem very well applied. And his eyes seemed odd. Only his right eye was moving, back and forth, back and forth, in some kind of a signal.

Toby looked down the clown's costume. On the ground near his huge feet were a few drops of blood.

Toby looked back up, into the clown's face.

The clown darted his eye back and forth again.

"See ya, kid."

Toby grinned.

He gave a little wave with his free hand, only waist high.

His mother did not see him.

Sixty-seven

Wednesday, Ambassador Teodoro Rinaldi walked into the V.I.P. lounge at San Francisco Airport, where his wife and son were waiting for him. He dropped his briefcase and put one arm around Toby and the other around Christina.

The family embraced wordlessly.

"Your luggage will be right up, sir," the stewardess said.

"I know." The Ambassador smiled at her. "Someone's downstairs watching for it."

Finally, Teddy said, "We might as well sit down while we're waiting. What's wrong with your feet?"

Christina dropped back down into her chair. "Plumb wore out. They'll be all better tomorrow."

Toby jumped onto the divan next to his father. "Fac' is," he said, "I'm hungry. Pizza!"

Again, Teddy put his arm around him.

Returning to the airport was not as difficult for Christina as she thought it would be. She had spent such awful hours there. But this time Toby was with her and they hadn't had to wait long for Teddy.

Christina and Teddy had talked at length on the telephone both Monday and Tuesday nights. Monday night Teddy told her Resolution 1176R had passed in the United Nations, with only nine no votes and one abstention—the United States. Tuesday Teddy told her Pat Skinner had been fired from the State Department.

"I guess Pat misread my face at some point," Teddy said.

To them both the grand news was that "the boss"

had endowed a chair of international diplomacy at Kennedy, provided Teddy be granted the chair for the first three years. Christina detected the kind hand of Ria Marti behind the endowment and the provision. Surely, "the boss" had not thought of it himself. Three years in Cambridge, living quietly with Teddy and Toby. . . .

Late Monday afternoon, from Fantazyland's parking lot, Christina had called Bernard Silvermine at the Red Star-Silvermine Motel.

"Mr. Silvermine? May I make a reservation for two, for tonight? In the name of Rinaldi—Christina Rinaldi and son, Toby. . . ."

Bernard Silvermine had a kilted bagpiper piping in the motel driveway when they arrived at dusk.

Tuesday and Wednesday, waiting for Teddy, playing around the motel pool, eating in the coffee shop, Toby told Christina some things about what he knew had happened.

His stories, of course, were childish. He was precise about some things: nearly being hit by a train, attacked by a shark in the river, falling down the side of Uncle Whimsy's Hat.

He was most vague about the kidnapper.

When she asked specific questions, Toby seemed to find it difficult to remember. How old was the kidnapper? Well, he was older than Dad—about fifty. Yes, he did limp. He had a wooden leg, you see, like a pirate. Glass eye? No, the man didn't have a glass eye. He said the man had said his name was O'Brien, and he lived on a ranch in Texas.

Christina had not told Teddy about The Hall of Knives—how, without thinking, without even knowing she was doing it, she had killed a man. She would tell him when he was rested. Or maybe never.

Now Toby was sitting on his legs on the airport divan, facing his father, jabbering about Fantazyland

and about many people and things that are not what they seem.

Smiling broadly, Teddy looked at Christina.

Christina asked, "Did Mrs. Brown send the carpets to the cleaning department at the museum, as I suggested?"

Teddy looked surprised. "Mrs. Brown?"

"Yes."

Teddy said, "Mrs. Brown isn't at the legation anymore."

"She isn't? Teddy!" Christina sat up in her chair. "Where's Mrs. Brown?"

Teddy's grin was the broadest she'd ever seen on his face. "Downstairs. She insisted on taking charge of our luggage herself. Don't know why she thinks any of it might get lost. . . ."

Toby said, "Yeaaaaaaa! Will she come to Fantazyland with us?"

Teddy said, "I don't think you could keep her away with a bazooka."

Toby said, "I can show you some marvelous things."

"I'm sure you can," his father said.

"I know Fantazyland pretty well now. Almost better than anybody, I bet."

Teddy look at Christina. "Maybe your mother doesn't feel like going back to Fantazyland."

Christina's stomach churned at the thought.

Teddy and Toby were looking at her, hoping she'd say yes.

She put out a hand to each of them.

"Anything to be together," she said.

THE WILD ONE

by
MARIANNE HARVEY
bestselling author of *The Dark Horseman*
and *The Proud Hunter*

Proud, beautiful Judith—raised by her stern grandmother on the savage Cornish coast—boldly abandoned herself to one man and sought solace in the arms of another. But only one man could tame her, could match her fiery spirit, could fulfill the passionate promise of rapturous, timeless love.

A Dell Book $2.95   (19207-2)

From the bestselling author of
Loving, The Promise, and Palomino

The RING

Danielle Steel

A DELL BOOK
$3.50   (17386-8)

A magnificent novel that spans this century's most
dramatic years, *The Ring* is the unforgettable story
of families driven apart by passion—and brought
together by enduring compassion and love.

At your local bookstore or use this handy coupon for ordering:

Dell Bestsellers

- ☐ **WHEN THE WIND BLOWS** by John Saul $3.50 (19857-7)
- ☐ **THY NEIGHBOR'S WIFE** by Gay Talese $3.95 (18689-7)
- ☐ **THE CRADLE WILL FALL**
  by Mary Higgins Clark $3.50 (11476-4)
- ☐ **RANDOM WINDS** by Belva Plain $3.50 (17158-X)
- ☐ **THE TRAITORS** by William Stuart Long $3.50 (18131-3)
- ☐ **BLOOD RED WIND** by Laurence Delaney ..$2.95 (10714-8)
- ☐ **LITTLE GLORIA . . . HAPPY AT LAST**
  by Barbara Goldsmith $3.50 (15109-0)
- ☐ **GYPSY FIRES** by Marianne Harvey $2.95 (12860-9)
- ☐ **NUMBER 1**
  by Billy Martin and Peter Golenbock $3.25 (16229-7)
- ☐ **FATHER'S DAYS** by Katherine Brady $2.95 (12475-1)
- ☐ **RIDE OUT THE STORM** by Aleen Malcolm ..$2.95 (17399-X)
- ☐ **A WOMAN OF TEXAS** by R.T. Stevens $2.95 (19555-1)
- ☐ **CHANGE OF HEART** by Sally Mandel $2.95 (11355-5)
- ☐ **THE WILD ONE** by Marianne Harvey $2.95 (19207-2)
- ☐ **THE PROUD HUNTER** by Marianne Harvey..$3.25 (17098-2)
- ☐ **SUFFER THE CHILDREN** by John Saul $2.95 (18293-X)
- ☐ **CRY FOR THE STRANGERS** by John Saul..$3.25 (11870-0)
- ☐ **COMES THE BLIND FURY** by John Saul $3.25 (11428-4)
- ☐ **THE FLOWERS OF THE FIELD**
  by Sarah Harrison $3.95 (12584-7)

At your local bookstore or use this handy coupon for ordering:

DELL BOOKS
P.O. BOX 1000, PINE BROOK, N.J. 07058

Please send me the books I have checked above. I am enclosing $_____
including 75¢ for the first book, 25¢ for each additional book up to $1.50 maximum
postage and handling charge.
Please send check or money order—no cash or C.O.D.s. *Please allow up to 8 weeks for
delivery.*

Mr./Mrs._____

Address_____

City_____ State/Zip_____